THIS BOOK BELONGS TO

. . . .

. . . .

A

MOLE

LIKE NO OTHER

Julia B. Grantham

A
MOLE
LIKE NO OTHER

Illustrated by
CAROL WELLART

First published in paperback by SDS Media LLP in 2021

ISBN: 9798694878722

To Sasha

Contents

Chapter One

The Morning of His Life

For as long as he could remember, the mole had been in the box. Dark and stuffy, tightly packed with old things that nobody wanted anymore: mismatched building blocks, cars without wheels, battered ballet shoes, torn books and bright plastic toys that came free with children's magazines. His nose – and a very sensitive one, if you must know! – was pressed against a smelly football boot. His body was squashed by a big yellow tractor.

Sometimes the mole had vague memories of another life – the bright light of day, sounds of laughter, fast moving cars on the wide roads, people's faces, unbroken toys and sweet-smelling flowers. But they were hidden so deep in his mind that he couldn't be sure whether this life had actually happened or he'd only imagined it.

The only other creature he could make out in the box was a small soft dinosaur to his left – still and unresponsive, probably believing itself to be completely extinct and ready to fossilize.

Fortunately, the mole knew better. His eyes were used to the dark and his mind was canny. He was resolved on viewing his life in the box as a hibernation (in simple words, a long winter sleep, but, you see, the mole did not fancy simple words and would never use a short word where a long one would do). He believed that there were better things in store for him and patiently waited for them to happen.

And one morning his patience was rewarded!

In all honesty, he didn't quite know what time of the day it was, for it was always dark in the box. But as this was the moment his adventures started, he decided to call it "morning". "The Morning of my Life" was how he referred to it ever after.

That morning the mole woke with a jolt. The box was rising up! It shook from side to side, forcing the mole's nose so tightly against the smelly football boot that he could hardly breathe. He held his breath for as long as he could, and, when he couldn't hold it any longer, he gasped. To his surprise, his ever-sensitive nose picked out some freshness in the air that brought a welcome relief from the smell of the old boot.

From this limited information the mole deduced that the box had been taken outside. Then it fell, landing with a 'thump' that pushed the yellow tractor an inch or two deeper into the box, pinning his body down even more firmly than before. But the mole didn't care.

'It's started!' he thought, excitedly. 'Things are going to change!'

Nothing troubled him anymore: the darkness, the stuffiness and the tightness of the box were now unimportant. Things were going to change! His adventures had begun!

The mole heard the thud of a heavy lid above his head, felt a sharp rumble beneath the box and they began to move.

The journey was short and soon the box was picked up again, carried into a place filled with many voices, positioned on a firm surface and –

OPENED!

At that moment the mole felt glad that his eyes were tiny and set deep inside his coat – for the light that filled the box when it was opened was unbelievably bright, much much brighter than he had ever remembered or, indeed, imagined.

While he squinted, gradually becoming used to the light, the things in the box around him started disappearing, picked out one after another by a pair of hands. The mole wiggled desperately, trying to get a better view, but the yellow tractor held him firmly in place and the smelly football boot kept his head in an awkward position, preventing him from seeing much.

All he could do was wait and listen.

"C'mon, Lorna!" the mole heard a boy call. "Hurry up, the fair has already started."

"Don't you tell ME," replied a girl in a squeaky voice that sounded familiar. "I told YOU we were gonna be late. It was YOU who went upstairs for *one last box*."

"Just wait until I sell all my stuff and make way more money than you!" shouted the boy and the mole heard the sound of a scuffle.

"You two!" a new, older voice interrupted. "You behave or you'll get no money to keep, neither of you, I'm telling you now!"

The mole lay in the box and couldn't wait to be picked out. When the dinosaur disappeared, he felt a little sad that he hadn't had the chance to say "Hello" or "Goodbye", but the next moment these thoughts vanished and he felt elated as the hand pulled the smelly boot away from his face.

'Fresh air!' thought the mole, taking a big breath.

Next – what joy! – the yellow tractor was lifted off his chest. The sense of weightlessness and freedom was so overwhelming that when, in turn, he himself was taken out of the box, his head was spinning, his heart singing and he believed he could fly!

Alas – Lorna's squeaky voice brought him crashing back to earth far too soon.

"Mum, do you think anybody would want to buy this ugly old mole?"

"Ah," the girl's mother waved her hand dismissively, "put him on the table all the same. You never know what people might fancy. We are definitely not taking anything back from here! You either sell your stuff, or it goes into the bin, mark my word!"

For the first time on this glorious morning the mole's insides were gripped with fear. The girl didn't like him! She thought him so ugly and repulsive that she didn't even want to place him on the table. A faint memory came to him, of a long time ago, in the life he wasn't sure he'd had, life before the box, when this very girl had described him with these very words – "an ugly old mole" and thrown him into the dark corner under her bed.

What if she was right?

What if nobody wanted him?

What if nobody would even look at him?

What if, at the end of this wonderful day, this day full of light and sound, this day of high hopes and great expectations, he would have to go back into the box and spend the rest of his life there?

Or worse still…

What if he were left in this hall and, after everyone else went home, thrown in the dustbin with the other rubbish?

Chapter Two

The Easter Fair

Gripped with panic, the mole's heart had stopped for a whole minute and then started again, racing fast and loud. He looked around, trying to understand better where he was and to make a plan how to avoid the bin at the end of the day. He was sitting in a line of toys, books, video games and clothes on a wide plastic table inside a large hall. There were other tables around, a stage at the far end and a long banner across the wall with something written on it in big red letters. The mole could read a little bit. He recognised many letters, like E and A, and S and T, but he was so upset right now that he was not able to put the letters together into words.

There were many people, large and small, moving between the tables, chatting happily, buying chocolate eggs and yellow daffodils in tiny brown pots, rummaging through books and toys on the stalls, sometimes choosing one or another but much more often leaving the stalls without taking out their money.

Desperately, the mole scanned the crowd with his tiny eyes for the ONE. The ONE customer who would choose him, pick him up, buy him, the ONE who would save him from going into the bin.

Lorna's words kept ringing in his ears: "Ugly old mole."

The more he thought about it, the more he remembered that a long time ago he was meant to have been Lorna's toy. He was her birthday present from an elderly aunt, but she hadn't liked him at all and threw him under the bed where he spent days, or maybe years. He remembered how the dust had slowly covered him from head to toe, getting thicker and thicker, like a grey fluffy blanket. He remembered how lonely he had felt and how badly he had wanted to be found and given back to little Lorna. But when, one day, a long brush had caught him and pulled him out, Lorna gave him only one look before throwing him into the box of unwanted things with those hurtful words "ugly old mole". And – just think about it! – he'd missed her all the time under the bed and wanted to play with her!

The mole was drowning in these unhappy memories that came back to him in a flood, until a customer approached their stall.

The football boots were first to go.

"Like new, just dirty," said Lorna's mum. "Only used once or twice."

'I know how new they are,' muttered the mole to himself, vividly remembering the nasty smell that ONE of them had made, pressed against his sensitive nose. 'Imagine what kind of odour the two of them together must produce!'

The yellow tractor also went quickly, together with an orange cement mixer and a blue digger.

Next was the turn of a whole lot of steam engines with smiling faces. They commanded a high price. 'How silly is that!' commented the mole, feeling very jealous of their apparent, but – in his opinion – undeserved popularity. However, he felt ashamed when each of the tiny engines whispered "Goodbye" to him as they disappeared into their buyer's thick plastic bag.

'They are rather nice and polite,' thought the mole, wishing now he'd got to know them better.

The fair was growing busier. The stream of customers at their stall became thick and steady. T-shirts, swimming costumes, Barbie dolls and video games were flying off the table, yet the mole remained.

No one had even picked him up to have a look. No one at all. They didn't even want to take him as a free gift (for he was now being offered as such to everyone by Lorna).

His spirit was sinking lower and lower and he closed his small beady eyes, for he couldn't bear scanning the room for the ONE anymore.

He felt desperate.

Sad, lonely and desperate.

When he heard a voice saying "Mummy, look!" the mole did not open his eyes.

He knew the voice was coming from the front of their stall, but he didn't want to know what the boy was admiring: the collection of football stickers or the last DVD remaining on the table. That is why he was astonished to feel himself being lifted in the air by small hands.

"Isn't he a bit babyish for you, Ashley?" said Lorna's mocking voice.

'Keep quiet, Lorna!' the mole wanted to scream, but instead closed his eyes even tighter, scared to spook away his luck.

"Oh, he is adorable," said a new grown-up voice, and the mole opened his eyes.

He was in the hands of a boy, who held him close to his face and looked at him intensely through a pair of glasses.

"Can we buy him?" the boy, whom Lorna had just called Ashley, asked the woman standing next to him. (His mother, deduced the mole.)

"Absolutely," was her response, "But wait…"

The mole closed his eyes again, dreading the worst – that she would think him ugly and change her mind.

"Look at that soft dinosaur. Isn't it a pair for the one you have?"

"Oh yes!" exclaimed Ashley, and the mole knew that he would be put back on the table and the dinosaur would be chosen instead.

But – no!

Ashley picked the dinosaur up with his free hand and brought her up so that she was right next to the mole. "Can we have her as well?" he asked, hesitantly.

"We can't leave her lying here alone, can we?" replied his mother, leaning in close and speaking in a whisper.

The mole heard Lorna's giggle from the other side of the stall. She asked: "Are you still playing with soft toys, Ashley?"

'Oh, please keep quiet, Lorna,' pleaded the mole silently, fearing that she might tease Ashley out of his determination to buy him and the dinosaur together, or even either of them.

"We are collecting them, especially the unusual ones," said Ashley's mother, with a little wink to her son. "And we've never ever seen a mole like this, or any mole at all for that matter. As for the dinosaur, we have her brother at home, so they will be happy to be reunited."

Lorna's mother laughed and a couple of pounds was handed over very quickly. Everyone seemed happy (except for Lorna's brother, who had lost his competition with Lorna on who would make the most money at the fair).

But the mole was happiest of them all.

He was chosen.

He was bought.

He was being carried away to his new home.

His adventures had truly begun!

Chapter Three

The Mole Gets a Name

Now the mole and the dinosaur rode in a car for the second time that day, but what a different journey this was! Instead of a car boot and the tightly packed box, they were comfortably seated on Ashley's lap, so that they could see the tops of the tall buildings and a little bit of the sky with low clouds passing by the window as the car made its way through the city.

After all the worries of the morning, the mole did not have any energy left for thinking. He sat there happily, enjoying the warmth of Ashley's hands holding him.
He breathed in the fresh smell of the mints from Ashley's pocket and the salty smell of the sea filling the car through the half-opened window on the mother's side.

For the first time in his life the mole felt safe and needed, and the feeling was so pleasant that his little face widened into a happy smile. He almost wanted to sing of his joy and excitement, but he wasn't a singing kind of mole.

He turned to his friend the dinosaur – for after everything they'd been through together, he considered her a friend – wanting to share his excitement, but she was fast asleep. The mole was quite surprised that she was able to sleep when there were so many new things to see.

They travelled for a long time. The tall buildings in the window were replaced by equally tall trees and the smell of the sea was succeeded by a mixture of countryside scents: sweet flowers, freshly cut grass and a hint of manure.

When the car turned into a driveway and stopped in front of a red-brick house, Ashley said, "Welcome home, you two. Come on, I want you to meet everyone."

Ashley took the mole and the dinosaur upstairs, into a large bright room at the end of a long corridor. Our mole loved it at first sight.

It had three windows with low wooden sills. 'Just the right height,' he thought, 'for sitting and watching everything that is going on outside.'

The windows looked out onto the front garden, with a big pond and an enormous weeping willow bending low over it. The mole instantly convinced himself that this was the best view in the house – and, in fact, he was absolutely right.

In the middle of the room stood a wide bed covered with a patchwork quilt of many colours. And in the middle of the quilt sat a small group of toys.

There were many other toys around the room but the mole immediately knew that the group on the bed were Ashley's closest friends and he set his heart on being seated there and nowhere else.

'Oh, what if I don't make it to the bed,' he started worrying at once, for he was a worrying kind of mole.

"Here, everybody," said Ashley. "I want you to meet new friends. I have a real surprise for you, Bronti! Meet your long-lost sister – Dina!"

The mole spotted, among the animals sitting on the bed, a soft dinosaur that was the spitting image of the one that had come from the fair with him. He had the same little face and looked at his sister with the same big eyes. 'Ah! They are twins!' deduced our mole in his head, as Ashley placed Dina next to her brother and they leant their long necks against each other.

The mole turned his attention to the other toys on the bed.

To the right of the dinosaurs sat two small dogs, both about the same size as our mole. One looked like a Labrador puppy, he was light brown in colour and had a collar round his neck with a name tag "Rusty". The other dog was the colour of chocolate and didn't wear a name tag. Both looked friendly, with keen interest in their eyes.

"These are Rusty and Rosie," Ashley introduced them. "They are very good dogs – kind and helpful."

'I can see it clearly,' thought the mole.

"This is Owlie," continued Ashley, pointing at a large grey owl with enormous blue eyes, pointy ear tufts and an impressive beak the colour of a fresh carrot. "She is incredibly clever and knows simply everything. She is very warm and cuddly too." (That wasn't surprising as there was a hot-water bottle hidden inside her, but, of course, the mole didn't know this.)

He looked into Owlie's round eyes, and she stared back at him with great intensity.

'Hmm...' he thought. 'It is surely a good thing to have someone clever for company, but I wonder... How can someone clever have such huge eyes?'

You see, the mole thought himself to be rather clever. In fact, ever since Lorna had called him "ugly" he'd consoled himself by remembering his shrewd mind. Being so intelligent (even if only in his own opinion) he also believed in keeping his ideas to himself and didn't like anybody to read his thoughts in his eyes. Therefore, it was really handy to have such tiny eyes well hidden in his thick fur. That is why he didn't believe that someone could be really clever with such gigantic bulging eyes.

'We'll see how clever she is,' he thought to himself, a little competitively.

Next to Owlie sat a big Teddy Bear. He was even bigger than the owl, who was not on the small side herself.

"This is Boris," said Ashley. "He comes from Russia. He is very strong and brave. I think you will become very good friends as he is the best bear in the world."

The mole was impressed with everything about Boris the Bear, from his size to the fact that he came from a foreign land, but he didn't have a chance to ponder upon it because Ashley brought him forward with the words:

"And this," continued Ashley, "is Moley."

With these words he placed the mole between the bear's paws so that Boris was now hugging him pretty tightly.

"There," said Ashley with a satisfied smile.

And that is how Moley got his name.

Chapter Four

First Impressions

At that moment Ashley's mother called him to lunch and he disappeared from the room.

"Well," said Moley, wiggling himself carefully out of Boris's warm embrace. "I am very glad to meet you all. That's for certain. You all seem to be very nice."

"TRRRRRRRRRRUE!" replied Boris the Bear in a big, low voice with a rolling "R" and a hard "T".

Moley, who had never heard a Russian accent before, jumped with fright. Boris spoke so loudly and his "R" was so long, that it sounded like a massive roar, although his face remained benign and friendly – not cross at all.

Still, Moley moved away from Boris just a little, to be on the safe side.

"Good to meet you, Moley," said the dinosaur called Bronti, turning towards Moley while remaining at his new sister's side. "Dina said that you hibernated with her in a dark box. Thank you for keeping her safe."

"Oh, it was nothing," replied Moley, meaning to say that there was *actually* nothing he had done to keep Dina safe. But it sounded as if he was saying it just to be polite and he felt a little embarrassed and blushed inwardly. Of course, no one could see him blushing because of the thick fur that covered his body, but his nose got a bit pinker than normal and he looked around nervously, worrying that the others had noticed.

The two dogs, Rusty and Rosie, moved closer to Moley, wagging their short tails.

"You are very welcome," they said in unison, then they continued talking over each other, both trying to be helpful and give Moley as much information as they could. "You will like it here. *It is a very good home.* The people who live here are Mummy, Daddy… *and Ashley!* They are called Mr and Mrs Richards. *And Ashley!* Yes, yes, and Ashley! *Ashley loves his toys very much.* He plays with us every day, even though he goes to school now! *He allows us to sleep on his bed!* The Richardses are all awfully good!"

Moley liked the sound of this and thought himself very lucky to have ended up in such a home. It was all turning out just as he dreamt! If he became friends with all these toys, it would be like a proper family!

His slight remaining worry was the owl, who made him feel a little uneasy with the silent gaze of her big round eyes. She watched him intently and without winking, but he wasn't able to read a single thought behind her steady gaze. 'Hmm...' said Moley to himself again, 'It seems that one *can* conceal one's thoughts, after all, even behind such enormously huge eyes. Interesting...'

He was fascinated by Owlie and wanted to impress her, to show her that he was worth talking to, and – perhaps – even becoming friends with.

Feeling slightly flustered but trying to hide it the best he could, Moley turned to the other toys on the bed. The pause in conversation was getting long and he needed to fill the silence.

"As I understand," he said in the calm and authoritative voice of a leader, for he couldn't help but behave like one wherever he went – he was that kind of mole, "you all know each other well, but Dina and I are new here. Why don't you tell us your stories? Who was the first to come to live in this house?"

For a few moments everyone looked at each other. It so happened that they had never discussed this topic before and didn't know the answer to Moley's question. After a while, Owlie spoke for the very first time in a voice no less calm and authoritative than Moley's: "I believe that would be me."

Everyone fell silent, turning their heads to her with the utmost attention and respect.

From that moment Moley knew there already was a leader in that room and – alas! – it wasn't him.

And again, he thought: 'Hmm... Obviously, keeping quiet sometimes can come in useful. If you don't rattle on endlessly, others will pay more attention to your every word when eventually you speak.'

The owl spoke again: "It is a truth universally acknowledged that a single owl in possession of a hot-water bottle must be in want of a home."

The mole was blown off his tiny feet by this sentence. He landed heavily on his back – his paws spread wide, his mouth open. He had always praised himself on his ability to speak eloquently and colourfully, BUT THIS...! He never imagined that one could speak in such a beautiful, almost musical way. With this impressive beginning, Owlie's reputation as the cleverest animal in the world was confirmed for Moley, and he thought that above everything else in the world, he wanted to win her respect and become her friend.

The owl continued.

Before she came to this house, she remembered hanging in a Chemist's window amongst the most boring and hideous of things: feeding bottles for babies, rows of soaps and dandruff shampoos, cough mixtures, plasters and nail clippers. She had a white doctor's hat pushed low on her head and a big red cross pinned to her chest. There was no one to talk to, no one even with whom to share a secret glance. All the owl could do was watch life in the street beyond the window.

The owl saw lots and lots of people passing by every day. Nobody ever looked at her window for longer than a moment. Some glanced at it and continued on their way, some had a face like they'd just remembered something and popped in through the shop door. Those who entered disappeared from Owlie's view, as the loop in her head attached to the hook in the window and prevented her from turning back to see what was happening behind her.

Not a single passer-by ever looked at Owlie herself, no one ever met her gaze, and no one, certainly, ever stopped for her.

Until one day...

Owlie wasn't in the habit of displaying her emotions, but at that moment Moley could hear a little creak in her otherwise calm voice.

One day, she continued, a young woman stopped in front of the window and looked right into the owl's eyes.

She looked and smiled and said: "Oh!" To tell the truth, Owlie couldn't hear a sound through the thick glass, but the young woman's mouth formed a perfect "O" shape, and the owl managed to figure out that the sound was, indeed – "Oh!"

The next thing Owlie knew, the young woman had disappeared inside the shop and then some strong hands pulled her off the hook, removed the stupid hat from her head and the sharp pin from her chest. And... lo and behold...

'Lo and behold!' repeated Moley in his head, in complete awe by now. 'My goodness! That owl can speak!'

...lo and behold, she was passed over the counter into the softest arms that she had ever known.

"Hello dear," said the young woman. "How cuddly and comforting you are! Just what I need right now."

At that point Owlie stopped telling her story, and looked around to check for the effect it was having on her audience.

Boris the Bear was asleep, along with the two dinosaurs whom he was hugging tightly (too tightly perhaps, but luckily the dinosaurs were very tough creatures).

The two dogs were still awake, listening with happy faces and wagging tails, in anticipation of a happy ending.

Moley was listening too, leaning forward to hear better, keeping his small beady eyes fixed on the owl, taking in every word and processing it keenly.

Owlie could see that in Moley she'd met a perceptive and attentive listener – despite the staggering difference in the size of their eyes – and was secretly pleased about it, for she was longing for someone who could appreciate her masterful storytelling and sophisticated language. But, as she wasn't in the habit of displaying her thoughts, she looked away from him, pretending to be indifferent.

For dramatic effect and in order to be asked to continue, Owlie finished the story abruptly in her calm voice: "And there you are, this is the end of my story."

To her surprise, Moley nodded his head in comprehension, but the dogs looked at each other in puzzlement.

"But... who was the young woman?" asked Rosie.

"I know!" Rusty barked brightly, excited with his idea. "It was Mummy and she brought Owlie home to Ashley!"

"Not quite," said the owl with a look of utmost importance, "for Ashley was not here yet."

"Where was he?" asked Rosie with even bigger surprise in her voice.

"He wasn't anywhere. He hadn't been born yet," replied Owlie, proudly observing the effect of her last words on the audience.

The dogs were speechless with shock. Moley managed to hide his astonishment reasonably well, thanks to his tiny eyes set deep in thick fur, but he WAS astonished. In his short life he had managed to figure out that things come and go. Clothes, boots, shoes, socks and even toys came from nowhere sometimes, and disappeared without a trace. But people?

From Owlie's words it turned out that people, just like toys, were not here all the time. They also came into the world from nowhere, and maybe – who knows? – maybe they also went? The thought was astounding and needed some thinking about. He was longing to talk to Owlie about it, but decided that today wasn't the time.

Happy with the effect her story had produced so far, the owl continued.

When Mummy (for it was indeed her) bought Owlie, she was expecting a child. She didn't feel very well at times, and a soft and cuddly owl with a hot-water bottle inside gave her just the comfort she needed. For Daddy wasn't always with her. He was a doctor and spent many days, nights and even weekends at the hospital treating his patients. Mummy spent her days studying psychology (another new long word for Moley) and many a long evening lay on her bed, hugging Owlie and watching television.

"After weeks and weeks of waiting," continued Owlie, "one day Mummy grabbed me in a hurry, we all got into Daddy's car and went to the hospital. But this time it wasn't for Daddy's work. This time it was for a very different reason."

Owlie paused again and looked around the room.

"That was how Ashley came into the family."

Owlie suddenly finished her story and closed her eyes for the first time since Moley had arrived, demonstrating clearly to everybody that she had nothing to add at that point. Moley was full of questions, but before he could open his mouth, Ashley ran into the room and scooped Bronti, Dina and Moley into his arms.

"I want you to meet Daddy, he's just come back from work," shouted Ashley excitedly and sprinted along the corridor and down the stairs – three steps at a time.

Chapter Five

Moley Meets Ludwig

The room Ashley brought them to was not very large but – really cosy – with an old brick fireplace and two leather sofas, covered in cushions of different colours and sizes, on either side of it. The ceiling was held up by dark wooden beams, and there were paintings on the walls and a rug on the floor. The fire burned bright and cheerful, wood crackling sometimes with a flair of sparks, filling the room with delightful warmth and a homely smell.

On one of the sofas sat a man with glasses on his nose and a gleaming screen in front of him. 'Mr Richards,' deduced Moley.

"Look, Dad," shouted Ashley happily, "Bronti has found his long-lost sister Dina."

The man peered over his glasses for a moment, and said: "Hah?"

"See, they look exactly the same! Dina is just a bit newer, maybe she wasn't played with much." Ashley laid the dinosaurs on his Father's lap.

"I see," replied Mr Richards rather absent-mindedly, returning his gaze to the screen.

"And now, meet Moley," announced Ashley, producing Moley from behind his back.

Moley spread his arms, as a star of the show might do, leaping on to the stage from the wings.

"Ta-da," shouted Ashley.

It had the desired effect – Dad looked up, chuckled and gave Moley his hand. It was too big for Moley to shake, but he squeezed Dad's thumb as hard as he could with his soft paws. Moley wanted to let him know how much he liked the house and the family that had adopted him and that he counted himself very lucky.

"He is quite a character, this one, isn't he?" said Dad.

Moley wasn't sure what this meant, but he liked the sound of it. 'I am quite a character,' he repeated to himself.

"Now, Ashley, let Daddy catch up on his Sunday papers," said Mummy, entering the room. "You know he was called to the hospital very early this morning, so he deserves some peace and quiet," she added, giving Ashley a little nudge towards the door.

"Can Moley stay here with you?" asked Ashley, picking up Bronti and Dina from Dad's lap.

"I can't see why not," answered Dad, returning to his screen. Ashley placed Moley on the cushion next to his father, who touched the screen with a finger, bringing it to life.

From his previous life Moley vaguely remembered "newspapers" as enormous sheets of paper covered in tiny letters, but all Mr Richards had in front of him was his glowing screen. He touched it with his finger lightly and the picture changed as if by magic. Moley sat so close to the screen that he could see everything even with his tiny eyes that were more used to the dark than the light. That afternoon Moley saw more fascinating pictures than he had seen in his entire life! He couldn't read much, for he wasn't a very good reader and only just managed the headlines, but in a couple of hours he'd learned lots and lots of new words and felt incredibly proud.

'There is so much in the world to see and learn,' he thought to himself, trying to remember the names of all the new places he'd read about.

After a couple of peaceful hours, which Moley enjoyed very much, the family decided to drive to the beach for a walk, and following a short frantic search for the car keys, they were all gone and Moley had the house to himself.

It was his time to explore.

Moley climbed down from the sofa and looked around, deciding which direction to take. He chose an arched opening that led from the lounge into a room with a big table in the middle and six chairs around it.

This room had a big window – from floor to ceiling, looking out onto the front garden with its pond, and by this window stood an enormous shiny bottle, as tall as a table and round like a car wheel. There were some twisted twigs sticking out of its top. Moley had never seen such enormous bottles before so he decided to investigate. He moved closer and then stopped, staggered to see an animal of some kind moving towards him from inside the bottle. This stranger was rather small and had a

pink nose. Moley waved at him tentatively and the stranger immediately waved back.

'Hmm, he looks like a mole,' thought Moley, slightly disappointed to discover that he wasn't the only mole in the house.

He moved closer and stretched out his right paw to shake the stranger's hand. The other mole moved his left paw forward.

'Rude,' thought Moley and quickly decided that he didn't like this other mole much. 'Unpleasant fellow,' he thought. 'No wonder he lives in a bottle. He wouldn't be nice company.'

Nevertheless, trying to be civil, Moley made as friendly a face as he could muster and said: "Good afternoon to you."

As he started speaking, the mole in the bottle said something too.

'Typical!' thought Moley, as he stopped himself mid-sentence, drew his paw to his ear and said: "Pardon, I didn't quite catch that."

To his annoyance the mole in the bottle did exactly the same.

'He is mocking me!' thought Moley, outraged. It was a sticky situation indeed, and Moley wasn't quite sure how to get himself out of it. He stared at the other mole in a challenging way, but the stranger only stared back. 'I'll show you what I'm made of,' thought Moley without breaking his stare, but the bottle mole looked just as determined. Moley stood his ground and wasn't going to give in, when he heard a snigger coming from the other side of a large window that stretched all the way to the floor.

Moley found himself in a pickle. On the one hand he didn't want to be the first to break the stand-off with the bottle-mole, on the other – his curiosity screamed at him to check out who was laughing outside.

Curiosity (of course) got the better of him and he ran over to the window and pressed his nose to the cold glass.

To tell the truth, Moley couldn't see very well with his tiny eyes in broad daylight, especially when the setting sun was shining right into them like today. He was a creature destined by nature to live underground in the dark and only to come into the daylight occasionally. But such a minor obstacle didn't stop Moley exploring whenever the opportunity came – day or night – for there were no limits to his inquisitiveness and desire to learn new things.

So, he had just pressed his nose to the glass, giving his eyes time to adjust to the sun, trying to see anything on the other side, when a loud tap right onto his nose made him jump and land on his bottom in the most undignified way.

"He is only a reflection, you know," said a large bird with a flat yellow beak on the other side of the window.

"Reflection?" repeated Moley. The word was familiar.

"Yep," said the bird by the window. "You see your reflection in the glass bottle, just like I see mine in still water, you silly little fellow."

'Reflection!' thought Moley and remembered what he knew about mirrors. Yes, mirrors did show back your own likeness, but Moley had never known that there were many different things that could reflect his face.

So, it turned out that all this time he'd been getting angry with his own reflection! He'd even started a staring contest with it! How silly was that?! He felt quite ashamed and made a promise to himself that, to avoid future embarrassment, from this point onwards he would always check whether he was truly angry with someone else or simply with himself.

Putting his excellent idea into practice, he peered at the figure behind the window: "You are not a reflection, are you?"

"Certainly not," said the bird. "I see my reflection in the pond often enough to know that I am not one!" He bowed his head a little. "I am Ludwig the Duck."

"I am Moley, the mole." He was proud to have a name at last. "Do you live out there?"

"I do," said Ludwig. "I live here in this garden with my wife. She is called Alexis, but she is rather busy now."

"You have a wife?" Moley's regard for the duck increased immensely, for he knew that only proper grown-ups had wives and husbands. To tell the truth, it wasn't at all surprising that Moley was impressed with his new acquaintance. Ludwig looked very handsome and very respectable indeed. His head and neck were of the deepest green, which gleamed with blue and purple in the light of the evening sun. His great chest was velvety brown, with a big white scar in the middle, undoubtedly, a reminder of some fierce battles. His posture was upright with his head held high, and his whole figure had a proud, dignified look, commanding attention.

"That scar of yours," asked Moley. "Is it from a battle?"

"Oh, yes," quacked Ludwig. "I have to fight with other ducks every spring. Everybody wants to live in this garden. It's got a sheltered pond for swimming, lots of flower beds with fat juicy slugs for eating, and – since this family moved in last year – plenty of the most delicious bread that they give us to snack on. From any duck's point of view, this garden is as good as it gets. So, you see, every spring I have to fight with other male ducks for the right to remain here. One day, when I am old, I'll lose and then another family will take this spot."

The last sentence made Moley sad, but Ludwig said it in a matter-of-fact manner and didn't seem upset. 'He knows that things come and go,' thought Moley, remembering his own realisation from earlier that day, 'and he accepts it'. It was a deep thought that required much more thinking, for which Moley didn't have time right now. He hoped to return to it later, but for now decided to remember never to take anything for granted.

"I wish I could come out into the garden with you," said Moley, wistfully. "It looks so beautiful out there."

"You are an indoors creature," replied Ludwig. "Every creature has its place. You – in the house. Me – in the garden. These rules should be obeyed. We are not the ones who created them and it is not up to us to change them."

Moley wanted to ask who had created these rules and why he had to obey them, but Ludwig flapped his wings as a "goodbye" and turned around, heading back to the pond.

Moley sat by the window thinking over and over all the deep thoughts of the day, not coming to many conclusions, but refusing to accept everything he'd learnt during this day as given. If he could get out of the box, he could get out of the house. If Ludwig got help from his friends, maybe he could stay in the garden forever. If he, Moley, tried hard enough, he could make all his dreams come true. As long as he didn't pick fights with the foes he created in his own head.

Moley's thoughts went round and round. They were deep and his ideas were big, but his head was rather small and it was getting heavier and heavier, until, quite unexpectedly, the mole was fast asleep on a fluffy rug by the big window, where Ashley found him some time later and took him to his bedroom.

From that day forward, every morning when Ashley carried him down to the kitchen for breakfast, Moley would hear a loud tap on the big window in the dining room and Ludwig's voice quacking: "Bread".

Mummy would laugh and rush to the window with a piece of bread, and Moley knew that Ludwig, his new friend, still reigned supreme in the garden.

Chapter Six

Danger in the Garden

One day, a couple of weeks after his arrival at the house, Moley sat on the windowsill in Ashley's bedroom and watched Mr Richards's car disappearing into the distance, taking him to work at the hospital and Ashley to his school. Mr Richards was a surgeon and worked very long hours, but tried to take Ashley to school if he could. Moley knew that in the mornings Mrs Richards always worked in her office on the ground floor that had a separate entrance from the drive. She was a counsellor. Patients came to her for help and advice every day and the door between her office and the rest of the house was firmly closed at all times.

Not expecting anything unusual to happen, Moley settled down on the windowsill for his mid-morning nap, but soon was woken by the most tremendous noise in the garden. He raised his head, sleepily focusing his gaze, and saw a man wearing a green shirt and green trousers going up and down the lawn with a very noisy machine. As Moley hadn't seen a lawn-mower before, he could not understand what was going on. Owlie told him what she knew:

This was a gardener, whom Mummy hired to cut the lawn in the front garden and clear the back garden. The family had only moved to this house last autumn, and they hadn't yet had a chance to tidy up. Although Mummy looked after the flowerbeds at the front of the house, the whole of the back garden was taken over by stinging nettles and thistles. So the gardener was taking care of it all.

Moley liked everything new, so he got down from the windowsill, snuck out of the bedroom and climbed downstairs to watch the gardener's work more closely from his favourite place by the big windows in the dining room. Interestingly, he'd now heard them called "French doors" by Mr Richards and "French windows" by Mrs Richards. It didn't make much difference to Moley whether they were windows or doors – they gave him an excellent observation spot, bringing him as close to the outside world as he could be. He settled there and watched.

The gardener wasn't a young man.

And he wasn't a fast worker either.

He slowly ran his mower along one length of the lawn... slowly emptied the basket full of grass into a big black sack... slowly dragged the sack along the lawn all the way to the compost heap behind the garage... slowly returned to his mower, whistling all the way, only to start the whole process again.

This unhurried work continued all morning and only one smallish lawn was done. With all the patience in the world (and our little mole believed that he had plenty of patience) Moley wished the gardener would hurry up. But the gardener didn't hurry with his monotonous work, and Moley eventually curled up by the French window and fell asleep, continuing his mid-morning nap, which had gradually become an early-afternoon one, thinking that he'd seen everything there was to see in the garden for that day.

But how wrong he was!

He woke up with a jolt, because someone was tapping on the window against his head with the utmost urgency and vigour.

"What? What?" cried out Moley, desperately trying to focus his sleepy eyes and recognising his friend Ludwig.

"Help us! Help us!" shouted Ludwig, flapping his wings in the most agitated way and stamping his orange webbed feet on the ground.

"What's wrong?" demanded Moley from his side of the window.

"The man! He's moved to the back garden. He's got this sharp wire on a stick with him that cuts everything. He is cutting all the stinging nettles right down to the roots!"

"But it sounds rather good to me," said Moley. "We'll have a tidy garden then."

"Good?" Ludwig dropped his beak open in disbelief. "Are you mad? Alexis is there! In the back garden. Under the elder tree. Hidden amongst the stinging nettles!"

"Why doesn't she move?"

Moley tried to be reasonable, but he really could not understand what all the commotion was about. He'd never met Ludwig's wife Alexis, for she was always "busy". To tell the truth, he'd even started to question her very existence. But now...what was all this to-do about? Why couldn't she move out of the way of the man's "wire on a stick"? (To you and me the "wire on a stick" is called "a strimmer" but we cannot expect a DUCK to know the right names for the gardening tools, can we?)

"You silly mole!" screamed Ludwig with indignation. "Of course, she can't move! She is sitting on the nest, sitting on her eggs, looking after our future babies!"

By now Moley, from his observations of little birds in the garden, knew enough about nests, eggs and babies, so he immediately understood the extreme danger of the situation.

"All aboard!" shouted Moley at the top of his voice.

(He wanted to shout something really brave and inspirational, like the captain of a pirate ship might shout rousing his crew for battle, but all he managed to come up with was "All aboard" – the call for late passengers to board the train. Afterwards he remembered this moment with a sense of great embarrassment, and would have much preferred to forget it altogether, but we cannot change the tale to please Moley, even if he says something silly.)

To his "All Aboard" no movement came from upstairs, and Moley guessed that at this moment of crisis he was on his own. There was no time to spare. He couldn't afford to climb all the way up the stairs to summon his friends, and had to act alone.

"Listen," he said to Ludwig. "Go quickly to the back garden and assess the situation."

"Do what?!" Ludwig turned his head sideways and looked straight at Moley with one eye. (He always did that when he was particularly puzzled.)

'Forget your clever words!' Moley thought, feeling annoyed with himself.

"Go to the back garden, check exactly where the man is, tell Alexis that help is coming and then come back and let me know what is going on. I'll be at the back door!" explained Moley.

Ludwig nodded and flew away, which was just as well, because he was a slow and clumsy walker.

Moley knew what he had to do.

In the back door of the house there was an old cat flap. Moley had been looking at it for ages. He'd dreamt of all the adventures and wonders of the big world that lay beyond the flap, but they were forbidden to him, for the flap was sealed off with two pieces of thick silver tape, criss-crossing it in both directions. Moley always thought of this big silver cross as a "Stop" sign and had never dared to challenge it. But today was different. He had to help his friend. He didn't know what exactly he could do, but he was determined to get to where his help was needed, and get there in time.

He rushed to the back door as quickly as he could and grabbed one corner of the sticky tape with his paws. He pulled and pulled with all his might and … nothing happened whatsoever. His small soft paws were losing out to the silver tape.

But suddenly Moley felt himself lifted into the air and heard the words: "Hold on tight, I will help you!" To his utter amazement Moley recognised Boris the Bear's voice, with its thick Russian accent. Boris was holding Moley in his arms and Moley reached for the corner of the tape, gripping as tightly as if his life depended on it.

"Raz, dva, tri," counted Boris in Russian, and to the count of three (that he pronounced as "tree") he pulled Moley (still holding the tape) across in one swift movement. For a moment Moley lost his bearings (with a bear!) but once he could see clearly again, one strip of the silver tape was in his paws and off the cat flap!

It was easy to remove the second strip for they knew now what they needed to do, and in no time the flap went loose and Moley could put his head through it.

"I'll hold it open for you," said Boris. "I am too big to go through the flap myself, but you can do what needs to be done on your own, I know. For you are a very special mole."

Without allowing him any time to reply, Boris pushed Moley through the flap and gave him a little wink when he landed safely on the ground.

"Thanks!" shouted Moley as he rushed away.

Chapter Seven

Moley to the Rescue

The garden was full of smells, sounds and colours. The sweet fragrance of roses climbing the walls on both sides of the back door made Moley a bit dizzy for a moment – or was it just the excitement of an adventure about to begin?

Any other day Moley would have stopped and reflected on the brilliance of his escape through the flap, but today there was no time. The sharp smell of freshly-cut grass and the noise of a strimmer in the back garden called him to action.

"Ludwig!" he shouted. "Where are you?"

For the first time in his life Moley saw Ludwig running. On his webbed feet he ran to the top of the garden steps and then flopped himself down from step to step, landing clumsily on each, not worrying at all about the dignity of his appearance.

"He's... getting... nearer," Ludwig breathed, one word per step. "He's... going... along... the hedge (the duck finally managed the steps) and it's only a hazel bush now between him and Alexis."

There was no time to waste, but what could they do?

"Take me there," commanded Moley, climbing on Ludwig's back.

"Hold on tight," shouted Ludwig and started running.

'Hold on tight,' thought Moley. 'For the second time today, I have been told to hold on tight. Lucky that I CAN hold on tight even though my paws are not all that long!' And he clasped his short soft paws around Ludwig's neck.

Ludwig jumped up the garden steps with much greater ease than he had jumped down and rushed across the back patch towards the elder tree.

The gardener was just a step away, but as he was wearing goggles to protect his eyes and large fluffy ear-muffs to protect his ears, he couldn't see or hear any goings-on around him, unless they were right under his purple nose.

Ludwig stopped by the tall clump of stinging nettles under the elder tree and Moley slipped off his back. He pushed apart the thick stems and … there she was.

Alexis, the Mother Duck.

She was real all right – real and remarkable.

She was sitting on her nest, clearly scared to death, but with such a look of steely determination to accept her fate rather than leave her unhatched children, that Moley felt a sudden spasm in his throat.

"Alexis, this is Moley," said Ludwig. "He will help us."

She lowered her head a little and looked at Moley with big eyes full of fear, but he noticed a tiny glimmer of hope hidden deep inside them.

'It is kind of her to rely upon me like that, but what can I do?' thought Moley in absolute desperation. 'She is well hidden here, but that is exactly the problem! She is hidden so well that the Gardener with his goggles and ear-muffs will kill her and destroy her nest in a second without even noticing it.'

An idea popped into Moley's head. Simple, but brilliant: 'Make him notice!'

"Ludwig, stand strong and flap your wings as much as you can," said Moley, loudly, over the noise of the spinning wire. "Make him notice us."

"Notice us? Are you mad? This mole is crazy, crazy!" cried Ludwig.

"Do as I tell you! NOW!" shouted Moley and threw himself on top of Alexis and her nest, his bright pink nose up in the air.

The strimmer was very near. The front rows of stinging nettles fell with a swish.

Ludwig was scared out of his wits, but he flapped his wings and quacked as loud as he could to attract the man's attention.

The nest was now practically exposed to the light of day.

Moley couldn't bear the noise of the approaching strimmer and the sun glaring brightly into his eyes, so he closed them, and was getting ready to accept his fate, just as Alexis was.

And then... the noise stopped. In the ringing silence Moley heard the man's voice: "What are you on about, you stupid bird?"

And the next moment: "Hold on, what have we got here?"

Moley opened his eyes and saw two big tanned hands stretching out towards him.

"What is this pink thing?" The man picked Moley up and noticed Alexis under him. "A duck on her nest!" he said in amazement. "Fancy that... I better go and report it."

The gardener held Moley in his coarse hand and carried him to the house (secretly celebrating yet another reason to stop working). He rang the doorbell and as soon as Mrs Richards, who fortunately had a short break between two clients, opened the door, he said, showing Moley to her: "Look what I've found in your back garden, Missus."

"Moley!" exclaimed she with amazement. "How did you get there?"

She took Moley from the gardener, who continued: "That's not all. This fella was sitting right on top of something else. Lucky, really. His pink nose caught my eye. If not, who knows what *could* have happened... Basically, you'd better come with me."

And he led Mummy to the back garden, right to the elder tree. Moley, still in her hand, saw Ludwig melting into the background nervously as they approached.

"A duck on her nest!" said Mummy. "Oh, my darling, I am so sorry we've ruined your hiding place."

She turned to the gardener: "Thank you for all your work today, but I am afraid you cannot continue here now."

"No, no, that won't do," answered the man. "You told me the full day – the full day I should be paid for."

"Yes, of course," answered Mummy shortly, "I will pay for a full day's work, thank you."

They returned to the house, the gardener was paid and quickly dispatched, and in the peace (at last) of the garden, Mummy looked at Moley inquisitively and asked again.

"How DID you get there, Moley?"

Moley knew that he could explain, but that was against the rules (for people think that toys cannot speak, and toys are bound to keep it secret that they can). So, he kept quiet.

"All right," said Mummy. "If you are so involved, let's go together and try to minimise the damage."

She pulled on a cardigan, placed Moley in her pocket in such a way that his head was sticking out and he could see everything, and picked up a pair of secateurs from a garden bench by the front door. With that she went to the back garden and started cutting off some branches from the elder tree and the hazel bush next to it. As she worked, she noticed Ludwig at a distance and said to him: "So Ludwig, this is where Alexis went. We were wondering where she'd gone."

From the branches Mummy started building a shelter around Alexis' nest.

"I am so sorry," she was saying to Alexis. "You must have been frightened to death when all this noise started around you this morning. But what a good mum you are, staying put and not moving a muscle, my brave girl."

Soon the job was done. The new shelter wasn't as good as the old one, but it was the best Mummy could do under the circumstances.

As she walked to the house, Moley was longing to tell her all about the events of the day and his own bravery and cleverness. But he felt that she already knew somehow. She put him on a soft cushion in the lounge and said with a knowing smile: "Enough adventures for one day, eh, Moley? Please stay put now. Unless, of course, someone else needs a rescue."

Chapter Eight

Moley Crosses the Road

After their big adventure Ludwig told every creature in the garden about Moley's intelligence, chivalry and valour. And now every time Moley appeared in a window, one bird or another would come to greet him and ask if he wanted anything. Moley seldom needed anything, but he liked giving birds little tasks, so that they could feel helpful. The birds happily brought to the bedroom window small daisy flowers that could be made into pretty chains, or sweet blackberries that all the toys – and Boris in particular – very much enjoyed. Moley felt very grateful to Boris for coming to help him in the crisis, and ever since thought of the big bear as his special friend.

When Mummy told Ashley about Moley's adventures in the garden, Ashley was very impressed, but also a little worried. With his dark fur Moley was not very noticeable on the garden soil and Ashley wanted to put it right. So, after an evening of whispered conversations with Mummy and some secret activity in her room, Ashley presented Moley with a piece of clothing in brightest yellow with shiny stripes criss-crossing on the back.

"This is your high-visibility jacket, Moley," said Ashley. "Make sure that you never leave home without it!"

Moley was extremely proud. He put his jacket on every time he planned a trip outdoors, but – between you and me – sometimes he put it on for no reason at all, just because it made him feel very important.

Of course, the most significant result of Moley's adventure in the garden was the cat flap.

For some reason nobody noticed that it had been undone, so it remained open and now Moley could go in and out of the house whenever he wanted. Well, almost whenever. He always checked that nobody could see him going outside, but with Daddy, Mummy and Ashley busy at work or at school most of the time, Moley had plenty of opportunities to explore the outside world.

The other toys didn't dare to sneak out with him. While Boris was far too big to fit through the flap, the other toys could have gone through it easily, even Owlie, at a push. But they found many excuses why not to do it. The dinosaurs informed Moley that they belonged to a different day and age and already felt out of place even being in Ashley's bedroom, so the wonders of the outside world might well be too much for them. The dogs claimed that they were there to guard the house and even a short trip outside would be seen by them as not carrying out their duties. The owl... Well, Moley wasn't sure what she thought. She hadn't asked him about the world outside in quite so many words, but he sensed her curiosity and – perhaps – a little bit of jealousy. Or was he just imagining it? In any case, Moley tried to share with his friends the stories of everything he was doing outside and never lost hope that he would get them into the garden sooner or later.

Every day Moley went to check on Alexis.

He added some leaves to her shelter, to replace the weathered ones, and even offered now and again to sit on the nest instead of her, so that she could have some time off – to eat a bite or two and have a quick swim in the pond. Alexis was truly grateful for his help and promised Moley she would let him play with all her ducklings when they hatched.

Well… that was the rub: when exactly were they going to hatch?

This question was troubling Moley more and more every day.

The problem was, whenever Moley sat on the nest he couldn't see or feel any eggs in it. The bottom of the nest was lined with a thick layer of Alexis' feathers, it was very soft and warm, but underneath it Moley couldn't feel anything. He didn't dare to dig down, in fear of damaging the eggs, but he started questioning their very existence after a few days.

Not being one to beat around the bush, he asked Alexis directly about it, but she gave him a little laugh and said: "I know what I'm doing, Moley, I am their mother." At first Moley was reassured, but the longer she sat on the nest the more he worried.

(He was actually a very impatient mole, as you might have guessed by now. And who could blame him? He'd done his waiting in the cardboard box and wasn't in the mood for more!)

One day he decided to talk about it to Owlie.

Ever since their first meeting he'd wanted to get to know her better and often went to her with one question or another. And, although the owl was always perfectly civil to him, she answered his questions briefly and he was left with the feeling that his company wasn't welcome. Eventually he came to the conclusion that she was better left alone, but his worries about Alexis and her unborn ducklings made him decide to try a conversation one more time.

"Owlie, you are a bird," he said. "So, tell me – as a bird – how long does it take for little ducklings to hatch?"

To tell the truth, Owlie had no idea. She was a bird all right, but she was a toy and didn't come from an egg herself, and had never met anybody who did. Of course, she could not admit her ignorance on such an important and thoroughly "birdy" matter, so she said with a significant expression on her face:

"It depends…"

None the wiser, Moley asked everyone about it and came to the conclusion that not one animal in Ashley's bedroom had the faintest idea on the topic.

He needed some expert help from birds who dealt with eggs every day! The idea came to him immediately – hens!

Every morning Moley was woken by a loud "Cock-A-Doodle-Doo" from the neighbours' garden over the road. It sounded like a cockerel (as indeed it was) and Moley deduced that where there is a cockerel there must be hens, and where there were hens there must be eggs. He thought that his logic was ironclad, and was determined to go on a big expedition to find the answer to his hatching question.

Next morning Moley rose with the first ray of sunlight. He knew that the Richardses would not be up for another hour or so, but still felt a little nervous, because he didn't want to be caught out of the house. He quickly pulled on his high-visibility jacket, quietly ran downstairs on his soft paws, and was through the cat flap in no time.

This early in the morning the garden was still sleepy – quiet and beautiful. The sun had only just peeped out shyly over the horizon, colouring a thin ribbon of the sky dusty pink, but the shadows under the trees lay dark and the grass sparkled with dew. The little birds were waking up, popping their heads out of their nests, but the silence had not yet been broken by their cheerful voices.

Moley made his way around the house and through the front garden, got soaked crossing the dew-clad lawn, but pressed on without stopping. He climbed between the iron bars of the gate that marked the entrance to the Richards's territory and stopped by the side of the road.

It was the first time in his entire life that he had stood alone by a road, intending to cross it.

Looking out of the window day after day, Moley had figured out pretty quickly that the road was not a place to take lightly. It looked smooth, like a grey river, calm and even inviting, but Moley knew it was dangerous, for he saw many fast cars driving along it, big heavy tractors making their way to the distant fields, and motorbikes flying by with a howling noise. Moley knew he had to be careful.

He stood a while by the side of the road, looking and listening. He turned his head carefully to look both ways and listened out for the sound of a car approaching from beyond the bend on the right. All was quiet. The neighbours' house stood just on the other side of the road, not far at all. All he needed to do was to cross the road, run across the lawn, go around the house – and find the chicken yard.

And yet Moley hesitated to make his move. That bend on the right troubled him, for he couldn't see around it and didn't feel that it was safe to cross without a proper check.

He was still undecided, weighing up his choices, when he heard a gentle throaty cooing from the pine tree on his left. A moment later a large wood pigeon landed on the fence next to Moley.

"Hello," he said. "You are up early. I am Gordon, by the way."

"I am Moley, pleased to meet you," replied Moley, always remembering his manners.

"Are you standing here enjoying the view of the road?" asked Gordon. "It is truly a very fine road, not too narrow and not too wide, and of a very pleasing shade of grey. I don't blame you for admiring it."

"A splendid road," replied Moley, who didn't want to start their acquaintance with a disagreement.

"As splendid a road as I've ever seen," echoed Gordon.

"I need to cross it, you know, but I cannot see beyond the bend."

"Do you want me to fly up and check?" asked Gordon, simply.

"That would be brilliant!" Moley's heart jumped with joy and he jumped with it. "Thank you!"

"No trouble at all," said Gordon, energetically flapping his wings and setting off.

From high above Gordon could see everything on the road for as far as a mile in both directions, but all he saw was the clear smooth surface of pleasing grey colour that he liked so much. He gave Moley the "all clear" and watched him tentatively taking his first step on the road.

Moley crossed in a straight line, looking in both directions and listening out all the way. Once on the other side he breathed a sigh of relief and congratulated himself silently. After all, crossing the road was not something that a mole like him does every day! With this happy thought he headed forward, around the neighbours' house and down to the chicken yard, surrounded by a mesh fence.

Chapter Nine

The Chicken Yard

Moley's arrival caused quite a stir. The hens closest to the mesh fence ran away, squawking and flapping their wings. Perhaps they thought he was a fox, or maybe they reacted this way to everything new. Moley expected that the cockerel would come out at once to protect his female companions, but it didn't happen. In fact, the cockerel was nowhere to be seen. Only after a while, when all the chickens had calmed down and started approaching the new visitor with curiosity, Moley noticed his head peeping cautiously from the open door of the hen-house.

"Good morning," said Moley in his friendliest voice and bowed ceremoniously to the chickens nearest to the fence. "Let me introduce myself. I am Moley, your neighbour from across the road."

Some chickens nodded their heads, others stared at him with blank eyes. You see, Moley didn't realise that many of them came from very distant countries, like Mexico and Brazil, and could not understand a word of English.

Upon hearing Moley's civilized address, the cockerel swiftly emerged from his hiding place and, pushing all the chickens aside, presented himself – chest forward – on the other side of the fence.

"Why, a good morrow to you, old chap," he said in a rather pompous drawling voice. "Let me introduce myself formally. My name is Viscount Charles Clumsy de Kerfuffle the Second and this is *my* hereditary estate."

His manners were so different to anything Moley had ever seen before, that for a moment he was quite taken aback. But he wasn't the kind of mole to be intimidated by a puffed-up chest and a long name! He quickly collected his wits and went straight to business.

"I am here with a question," said Moley, purposefully. "It is a rather delicate matter, but I hope you will be able to help me. You, chickens, always deal with eggs, and that is why I came to you with this problem. We have a duck in our garden, you see... She's got a nest and has been sitting on it for ages. I wonder if she's been sitting there too long. I cannot see any eggs in the nest. To cut a long story short – how long should a bird sit on the nest before the babies are hatched?"

Moley made the whole speech in one breath and afterwards looked at his audience expectantly. But all he observed was a round of blank looks. The thing, which Moley didn't know, was that these chickens laid eggs, but never sat on them to have chicks. They were "egg chickens" and had absolutely no idea how chicks came into this world. Viscount Charles Clumsy de... Oh! For goodness sake – THE COCKEREL – didn't like to admit his ignorance on such an important matter, and so he puffed up his chest even more and stated that he could not possibly answer such a question, for these matters were chicken's professional secret and not for sharing. Despite this pompous display, it was clear as day to Moley that all his haughty pretence was there to hide the simple truth that no-one in the chicken yard knew the answer to this question.

With great disappointment he turned around to go back home and spotted Gordon, the wood pigeon who had helped him to cross the road earlier, sitting on the fence not very far from their gathering.

Gordon looked at Moley with a twinkle in his eyes, clearly finding the whole situation amusing.

Moley looked up at him: "Maybe you can help, noble pigeon?"

"Noble pigeon?!" exclaimed Charles the Cockerel, at the top of his voice. "What a strange way to address a wood pigeon! No, not strange! Disgraceful! Don't you know that no-one from the woods can be noble?! They are all wild barbarians in the forest! Peasants and pheasants! The only noble bird in the whole world is the cockerel, and you are lucky that I've demonstrated such affability, such condescension as to speak to you at all!"

That was too much!

That was too much!

"Pah!" said Moley. "Lucky? Of course, I am lucky to see you. Lucky that you've managed to drag yourself here on your shaking legs, after hiding behind your hens, like a .... CHICKEN!"

The insult hit a sore spot. The cockerel's eyes turned bloodshot, his tail opened like a fan, he flapped his wings, and rushed, head down, to attack Moley.

In his rage he'd completely forgotten the mesh fence that stood between them! He ran straight into it and bounced back with a ferocious force. Viscount Charles Clumsy de Kerfuffle the Second landed on his back, kicking his legs in the air and hitting the ground with his wings.

"Pathetic," concluded Gordon, matter-of-factly.

Moley watched for a little while as the chickens helped the cockerel back on his feet and escorted him to the hen-house, clucking and fussing all the way, before he turned again to Gordon. "Do you know how long it takes chicks to come out of their eggs?"

"Three weeks," replied the pigeon, simply.

Moley knew that a week had seven days and figured out that three times seven was a lot of days, even though he couldn't say exactly how many. What he didn't know was that Gordon was a straightforward bird. He answered the questions that were asked, and only them. Moley asked him about chicks and he answered about chicks, not ducklings. But this little detail had escaped Moley's notice and he thought that his theory was confirmed.

"I knew it!" he exclaimed. "I knew she'd been on her nest for far too long. She's been sitting on her eggs much longer than that."

"Well," said Gordon, "you get a brooding chicken sometimes. She'll sit on the nest forever, even if it's empty. She just wants to have chicks so much – she can't accept the fact that they are not there."

"Yes, that's it!" cried Moley, quickly jumping to a conclusion. "It is exactly what's happening to Alexis."

Gordon didn't argue, and didn't ask any questions. He always believed that he would be told things he needed to know, and if he wasn't told – then he didn't need to know them. He just blinked, looking at Moley with one eye, and kept quiet.

"Thank you very much," said Moley. "I must rush back and do something about it."

He said goodbye to the chickens (the cockerel was nowhere to be seen), hurried along the mesh fence, made his way around the neighbours' house, crossed the road with Gordon's help as before, pushed himself between the bars of the tall gate, and ran home as fast as he could on his short legs. He just managed to make it through the cat flap and started climbing the stairs when he heard the alarm clock going off in Ashley's parents' bedroom.

Chapter Ten

Moley is Looking for Options

Moley had only just managed to reach the landing when he heard Mr Richards's steps approaching from the main bedroom. Moley only had time to throw himself flat on the floor, pretending he'd been there since last night. Ashley's dad passed Moley without noticing (as most dads would do).

Moley had just managed a few steps towards Ashley's bedroom when he heard Mrs Richards rushing down the corridor and had to freeze again. She spotted him at once, and – with "Oh, Moley, what are you doing here?" – picked him up and continued on her way to Ashley's room.

"Who's a sleepyhead?" she called, opening the door. "Look who I've got here. It looks like our Moley has been busy this morning. He was waiting for you on the landing, ready for a new day." Ashley opened his eyes, hugged Moley, kicked his blanket off and the morning rolled ahead in its usual "weekday-morning" way.

Moley often heard that people hated mornings. He never could understand that. For him the beginning of each new day was a little miracle. The world outside was becoming brighter, louder and busier by the minute with everything coming back to life after the sombre darkness of the night. The house was all hustle and bustle, people rushed around, tripping over each other, packed their bags, swallowed their breakfasts in a hurry, hugged and kissed by the door as a new day of adventures and discoveries began to unfold. What's not to like?

Once Mr Richards had left for work, taking Ashley to drop him off at school, and Mrs Richards disappeared into the annex office, getting ready for her first client of the day, Moley called an emergency meeting of the toys, to discuss – as he described it – "the situation".

"We have a brooding duck on our hands," he proclaimed without any warning.

His audience gasped. To tell the truth, none of them knew what it meant, but it sounded so grave and important that they couldn't help but fret. Moley, after making his shocking announcement and ensuring that everyone's attention was on him, proceeded to describe his morning at the chicken yard and what he'd learnt there.

"We need to decide how to help Alexis," he concluded.

"Why do we need to help her?" enquired one of the little dogs, Rosie. "Surely, one day she will understand that there are not to be any babies, and will leave the nest herself."

"But what if she doesn't? I've heard," – and we know that he'd only heard it that very morning from Gordon, – "that sometimes a bird can spend weeks on an empty nest, and with Alexis being on the ground and so exposed, she is in constant danger."

"Then we should talk to Ludwig," suggested Rusty. "He surely should know whether there are any eggs in the nest."

Moley was close to losing his temper: "There are none, I've told you, and if you –"

"Rusty is right," interrupted Boris, in his big low voice. "Whatever the situation, we should first talk to Ludwig. He is her husband, don't forget."

All the other animals nodded their heads in agreement and only Owlie did not as much as blink an eye. 'I wish I knew what she was thinking,' thought Moley to himself, then said aloud: "Fine" and shrugged his shoulders. He didn't have much hope. After all, he knew Ludwig better than anyone else in the room and (between you and me) didn't have a very high opinion of his intelligence.

The opportunity to talk to Ludwig presented itself later that morning.

Moley was sitting by the open window in Ashley's bedroom when he saw a duck's tail floating above the water in the pond. At first Moley was sure this was Ludwig, but quickly he noticed three more ducks diving for food in the same pond, and, by the look of it, enjoying themselves very much. They dived and splashed water around themselves, beating their wings vigorously, sending fountains of bright sparkles into the air, and then dived again, popping their heads down, tails bobbing above the surface like oversized fishing floats. Being unsure which tail belonged to Ludwig, Moley called for him several times, trying to catch the ducks at the brief moments between their dives, and eventually, albeit somewhat reluctantly, Ludwig left the pond and came to the house, looking up at Moley in his first-floor window. You see, Ludwig felt very obliged to Moley for everything he'd done for his family and couldn't say "no" to his friend's request.

However, Moley had just started asking his question when Ludwig cut him short, beating his wings and rising on his tiptoes.

"Stop right there and don't say a word more. I know nothing about eggs and babies. It is not a male thing to be involved in such matters! It is a female thing – she knows what she is doing, and I don't interfere at all. It is not my job. Now, excuse me, I have to go and chat with my mates. We're having a get-together today, can't you see?"

With these words he rushed away, waddling side-to-side, and joined the other male ducks, who by now had got themselves out of the pond and sat in a tight group on the bank, cleaning their feathers and pushing their chests out.

'Funny,' thought Moley. 'In early spring he fights with these very "mates" most fiercely, and doesn't allow them anywhere near his wife and his pond, but as soon as their wives are busy on their nests, the male ducks suddenly become best of friends, and spend time together as if the fighting had never happened.'

Smiling to himself and shaking his head in disbelief, Moley turned to Owlie, who was sitting on Ashley's bed by the window and had heard the whole conversation: "So... what do you think of his answer?"

"Absolutely barbaric," was her short reply.

Seeing Moley's puzzled look, she elaborated: "Him." Owlie pointed with her head in the direction of disappearing Ludwig. "What does he think this is? The eighteenth century?"

"Well, I suppose he is only a duck," replied Moley. "They haven't changed much since the eighteenth century."

Owlie didn't say anything to that and after waiting awhile, Moley decided to prompt her. "What shall we do now?"

"We need to speak to her," said Owlie.

She paused and thought a little. Then added: "But she is in distress."

Pause.

"We need to tread carefully."

Pause.

"I've learnt a lot of psychology, when I lived in Mummy's room."

Pause.

74

Conclusion: "Alexis needs counselling."

"Counselling" wasn't a new word for Moley. He'd heard Mrs Richards use it plenty of times when talking to Mr Richards about her work.

"Oh," said he. "I would love to do counselling."

"*Do* counselling!" Owlie's hoot sounded like a laugh. "You cannot just *do* counselling. You need to study a lot for that. I learnt it all with Mummy when we did our psychology degree. It took us a very long time!"

Studying for a long time was not in Moley's plans (or habits). He was the kind of mole who liked to act swiftly and wanted to see the results the very same moment. He didn't like the sound of this "psychology".

"Can't we go to Mr Richards's medicine cabinet instead, and find some sort of a tablet to give her?" he asked, rather pleased with his splendid idea.

"Typical!" exclaimed Owlie. "Doctor's view! Give them a pill! For your information, psychological

problems cannot be sorted out by medication only. They need to be addressed gradually, by changing of one's thinking and attitudes."

Owlie repeated the words she'd heard many times in Mr and Mrs Richards's discussions on the topic. She didn't quite understand them, but had always been impressed by their sound and wanted to use them at the right moment. How pleased she was that this moment had finally arrived and she could show off her erudition.

To tell the truth, Moley was duly impressed. After such a tirade he could not argue with Owlie any further. Plus, he remembered that Mr Richards's medicine cabinet was always locked and they didn't have the key.

So, it had to be counselling after all, and Moley was not the one who could deliver it. The question was – who could?

Moley looked at Owlie and she looked back at him with her large protuberant eyes.

After a few moment's silence, she exclaimed: "Alright, alright, I'll do it! I can't leave a fellow bird in distress without relief. It is my duty, I suppose, to help."

Chapter Eleven

Owlie the Counsellor

Early next morning, while the family was still asleep, Moley (wearing his high-visibility jacket, of course) and Owlie crept down the stairs, and made their way to the cat flap. Moley pushed his way through and held it open so that Owlie, who had to practically fold herself in two, could climb out. They made their way to the back garden and Moley led Owlie to Alexis.

The Mother-Duck was sitting on her nest with her usual look of serene but determined resolution. Moley introduced Owlie to her and sat aside, leaving them to speak in private. To be perfectly honest, he still could hear the conversation as moles have very acute hearing, but he didn't dare to move any farther away, in case his help might be needed.

"How are you today, Alexis?" started Owlie.

"I am very well, thank you," replied Alexis politely. "It is awfully nice of you to come to see me," she continued, sounding more and more excited. "It can be a very boring job sitting on the nest day after day, and night after night. I don't have many visitors, even my husband rarely pops here to see me. He, of course, was here by my side last week when I was in danger. I suppose you've heard all about it from my friend Moley?"

"Indeed."

Owlie was a little taken aback. She had planned to be the main speaker in the conversation and wasn't ready for such an enthusiastic response. She expected that Alexis would be unhappy and shy, and that she, Owlie, would have to drag every word out of her. But Alexis seemed very pleased to have someone to talk to, and couldn't keep quiet after her long solitude.

"Indeed, you would know about all the goings-on in the garden from Moley, wouldn't you? Oh, he is such a special friend of mine, he saved me, you know... He is simply wonderful, a very special mole, very special indeed. And he comes to sit on the nest for me, you know, so that I can have a bite to eat and a little dip in the pond –"

"Yes, yes, the nest," interrupted Owlie, a little irritably. "That's what I wanted to talk to you about –"

"It is quite exposed, I know," interrupted Alexis in turn. "But it is still better than it would have been if Moley hadn't been here in time. It is quite visible, but my feathers are so much like the earth and the brown leaves, that I don't think anyone can see me, unless they know I am here. Mummy comes every day to add some branches for my shelter, and it is all quite manageable, you know."

"But your nest –" Owlie tried to put a word in...

"Oh, the nest itself is very comfortable, I've done a really good job this year. It is so soft and deep and well-concealed. My babies will be nice and comfy here when they hatch."

"This is the point!" Owlie almost shouted now. "Your babies! When –"

"Oh, not long now. I cannot say exactly, they often have their own clock and know when it is their time to come into the world, but I feel that it won't be long. You are very welcome to come and look at them when they are hatched. You are a bird too, after all, you must love the little ones. Ducklings, that is the word for my babies, what is the word for yours? Owl-chicks, or owlings? Looking at you – you are so big and fluffy and look so warm. Could you possibly sit on the nest just for a moment? I know Moley is very kind and always ready to do it for me, but he is quite a bit smaller than you, and my babies need all the warmth they can get right now. If you'll oblige me and sit just for a moment here, I will have a little breakfast. I know that Mummy left some bread for me by the French windows."

With these words, Alexis firmly pulled Owlie's wing with her strong beak. Before she knew it, the owl was sitting on the nest, with the duck rushing away. Owlie's round eyes almost popped out with shock and indignation. For once in her life she was lost for words.

Moley, trying to suppress his smile, gradually moved into Owlie's view.

"Well?" he asked, desperately attempting to look serious.

"I will NEVER do counselling again!" said Owlie abruptly, and turned her head away from him.

Owlie cut such a comical figure, sitting on the nest all puffed up and fuming, that Moley could not suppress his laughter any more. It escaped his throat as a tiny squeak at first, but soon he was laughing out loud, holding his sides and shaking his head. He laughed, and laughed, and

laughed, until there was no more laughter left in him, and then he stopped and felt really awful. After all, it was he who had asked Owlie for help, it was he who brought her here. It wasn't a very nice thing to do to laugh at her after that.

"Sorry, Owlie, I shouldn't have laughed like that," he said, but Owlie did not turn her head. She looked away from him, in stony silence.

Moley felt sick. He knew he'd hurt her feelings, and wasn't sure how to make it better.

He apologised a couple more times, with no effect.

In silence they sat by the nest, and in silence Owlie climbed off it when Alexis returned. In silence she walked towards the house, Moley in her wake, ashamed of himself, waving a quick goodbye to Alexis.

They got back to the house through the cat flap, walked up the stairs and were just about to enter Ashley's bedroom, when Moley decided to make another attempt to make things better.

"Owlie," he said, "honestly, I didn't mean to hurt your feelings. I know you tried your best, but counselling is clearly not an easy thing to do…"

He realised he shouldn't have said that

when Owlie looked down at him with her huge eyes and two tears
dropped from them on top of his head. One from each eye. Still with no
words, Owlie pushed the door open, went into the bedroom, flapped
her wings and hopped onto Ashley's bed, nestling herself by his side.

Chapter Twelve

Moley is All Shaken Up

Although all the toys asked Moley and Owlie about their expedition, the two didn't say much. Or rather Owlie didn't say anything at all, and Moley answered with brief non-committal exclamations along the lines of "it was fine" and "all went well". It could not escape anybody's notice that there was something odd going on between Moley and Owlie, and the atmosphere in Ashley's bedroom quickly became heavy with unspoken bitterness and unhappiness.

Moley tried a few more times to apologise to Owlie when nobody was listening, to no avail. Every time he opened his mouth, trying to speak to her, she turned her head away from him and wouldn't turn back until Moley left her side.

The other toys did not want to take sides and preferred to talk in hushed tones among themselves, rather than with either of the fallen-out friends.

Moley felt guilty and lonely. He'd risked his friendship with Owlie, and for what? The "Alexis problem" had not changed at all, and instead of moving things forward, it seemed all he'd achieved was to make his life in the bedroom unbearable. His way of coping with this difficult situation was to try to escape it as often as he could. At every opportunity, over the next few days, he would put on his high-visibility jacket and run to the garden to spend time with his friends there, who talked to him and loved him no matter what.

The ducklings still hadn't hatched, and Moley noticed that even Mrs Richards was worried. She talked to Mr Richards about it a couple of times (in a low voice because they hadn't told Ashley about the nest). Observing her mood keenly, Moley came to the conclusion that Mummy also suspected the nest to be empty.

Despite all that, he hadn't given up on helping Alexis, and he still went to the nest every day, guarding it while Alexis had a little break. She really appreciated Moley's help and left the nest to his care for longer and longer every day. It was a little boring to sit there on his own, with no one to talk to, but then again, he didn't have many friends to talk to in the bedroom either. At least on the nest he felt himself useful.

He was sitting on the nest one Friday afternoon mulling over these unhappy thoughts, turning them in his head over and over, when he felt the ground under him moving a little.

'Earthquake!' was Moley's first thought. Only the night before he was sitting in the lounge with Ashley watching a programme on BBC2 about earthquakes and it had left a lasting impression on his impressionable mind.

"Alexis, come back!" he shouted. "Earthquake!"

He spread his paws, pushing hard into both sides of the nest, expecting another shake, and, sure enough, it came! He felt a strong push into his back and heard a loud crack.

'The earth is splitting!' thought Moley, his imagination painting a gruesome picture of a deep crack in the earth's surface going right through the Richards's garden and the nest.

"Help!" he shouted, but no help came.

Instead he felt the pushing into his back becoming more persistent, heard another crack and … a squeak.

Moley turned his head very slowly and saw two tiny bright eyes looking at him from the depth of the nest. A duckling?! How did he get there?

Moley didn't have time to think, because the fluff and feathers that lined the bottom of the nest moved – and another pair of eyes stared at him from below.

"Qua-mama," squeaked the ducklings in unison.

Moley thought he was worried about the earthquake, but that was nothing compared to the panic he felt when he saw two baby ducklings looking up at him and calling him "Mama".

"ALEXIS!!! COME BACK!" he shouted at the top of his lungs. "LUDWIG! SOMEONE! COME HERE!"

He heard a rustle of wings over his head and Gordon landed gracefully on the branch of an elder tree.

"I see congratulations are in order, Moley," he said with a twinkle in his eye. "Your babies have started hatching."

"Gordon, pleeease," Moley pleaded. "It's not the right time for jokes! Pleeeeeeease, find these irresponsible parents and bring them here, I have no clue what to do!"

"I shall," said Gordon. "What you need to do for now is to cover them with your body as best you can. I'll be back shortly."

He took off in the direction of the big pond in the front garden.

Moley spread his arms and legs, covering the ducklings with his little body and felt another crack and a push and then another. It was lucky that the newborn ducklings were very small and Moley still could cover them, but what if there were many more to come? Time dragged really slowly for Moley, but at last he heard a loud quack and Alexis landed heavily beside the nest.

"Moley!" she said. "You are indeed our saviour! How lucky it is that you were on the nest! But move over now, I'll do the rest."

With these words she pinched his paw with her strong beak and pulled him off the nest.

"Ouch," said Moley, for Alexis could be a little rough when she was preoccupied with something.

She looked into the nest and nodded: "They look alright. I think there are more to come."

She settled herself on top of the nest and turned to Moley:

"I am so sorry, Moley, I got it wrong. I thought they had another day or two to go and tried to enjoy my last days of carefree life. My life will change now they've come."

"Alexis," said Moley, "you were always right – there WERE eggs in your nest! Why didn't I believe you?!"

"I always say – trust the experts," said Gordon, who had just come back from his short expedition, with Ludwig in his wake.

"Yeah," nodded Moley, thoughtfully. "It is not always easy for me. I never believe anything until I can see it with my own eyes."

"That can be a problem," said Gordon, winking with both eyes.

Moley never quite understood whether Gordon was being serious or was teasing him, but now was not the right time for such deep contemplations. The ducklings were here and that was all that mattered!

Moley stayed by the nest for as long as he could. It was so nice to sit there on the warm grass, chatting with Ludwig, Gordon and Alexis, listening to high-pitch squeaks coming from the nest, but when the sun touched the top branches of the elder tree, Moley knew it was time to go back to the bedroom, to be there for Ashley's return from school. Next day was Saturday, with the Richards family all at home and Moley was sad to think that he would not be able to sneak out of the house to see the ducklings.

"I'll come as soon as I can," he said and turned his steps towards the back door.

He arrived back in Ashley's bedroom in the best of spirits. Somehow, he believed that the news about the ducklings would make things between him and Owlie fine again. But he was wrong.

He rushed into the bedroom, exclaiming excitedly: "I've got news!", only to be shushed by Rusty and Rosie, who sat on both sides of Owlie:

"Shhhhh! Owlie is asleep, she didn't rest well last night. Let her catch up on her sleep."

Moley felt deflated like a burst balloon. He had such wonderful news, he wanted to shout about it from the rooftops, and – what? He would have to tell it in a whisper, because Owlie didn't sleep well last night?

"She never sleeps at night anyway," he muttered to himself. "She is an OWL, for goodness sake!"

Rather than sharing his exciting news in a whisper he quickly convinced himself that nobody in the bedroom cared about the ducks anyway, and curled up in the corner, away from the other toys, sulking.

Chapter Thirteen

Meet the Ducklings

On Saturday morning, when the sun was particularly high, and the garden looked particularly inviting, Ashley decided to take all his favourite toys outside. He put Bronti and Dina, Rosie and Rusty, Owlie and Moley in the large wicker basket that normally stood by the fireplace, picked up Boris the Bear with his free arm, and ran out into the garden. There he placed all the toys on the bench neatly and went away to explore the garden.

Moley sat on the bench squinting at the bright sun, enjoying the sounds and smells of the garden, almost dozing off, when Ashley's loud cry made him jump.

"Mummy, Daddy!" shouted Ashley. "We have a duck on a nest in the back garden."

Mummy, who was kneeling by the flowerbed wearing gardening gloves, weeding, got up quickly and ran towards Ashley.

"I know, sweetie pie, I know," she said to him soothingly. "Don't disturb her. She's been there a while and I am afraid there are no eggs in her nest."

"Of course, there are no eggs!" replied Ashley excitedly. "There are ducklings!"

"What do you mean? Are you sure? Have you seen them?" Mummy was showering him with questions as they went to the back garden together.

Moley was ready to run after them, but in broad daylight, with the whole family in the garden, he had to stay put. He looked around at the other toys, anticipating their surprise, and was just about to tell them how the ducklings started hatching while he was sitting on the nest the day before, when, just before he opened his mouth, Owlie spoke.

"Well," said Owlie, not to anyone in particular, staring unblinkingly into the space above their heads. "I am glad to hear the news, I am sure. It is always good to know that one's efforts were not in vain. I spent quite a bit of time on that nest, you know." She turned her gaze to the toys.

The toys were so happy that Owlie had broken her silence that they hugged her and each other, congratulating her on this happy event. But when Moley turned to Owlie with his arms outstretched, she moved away. She'd broken her silence, but not for him. He wasn't forgiven.

Moley hung his head and moved to the other side of the bench. Alone. His mood ruined, his body heavy with sadness. But a moment later he felt a big paw on his shoulder, and Boris' deep voice said, "Well done, my friend. It wouldn't have happened without you."

Moley looked at him gratefully. He didn't want to blow his own trumpet, but he was hurt by everyone forgetting his role in saving Alexis and helping her with the nest. It was good to know that at least Boris remembered.

Moley sat next to his big friend, thinking about all that had happened to him in these last two days, hoping to see all the ducklings sooner rather than later, when Mummy and Ashley emerged from behind the corner with broad smiles on their faces.

"Can I show the new ducklings to all my toys, Mum?" asked Ashley.

"Maybe all your toys would be too much for them and their mother right now," answered Mummy. "She is very protective of her babies and you don't want to stress her out. But one fellow, I guess, wants to see them all very much."

With these words Mummy picked Moley from the bench and passed him to Ashley.

"Moley, do you want to see Alexis and her baby ducklings?" asked Ashley, running around the corner with Moley in his hand.

"I do, I do," Moley wanted to shout, but he managed to bite his tongue just in time.

Alexis was sitting on the nest as always. Someone who hadn't known her as well as Moley had, wouldn't have noticed any difference. But Moley saw that her serene expression had changed to a very anxious one. She looked nervous and scanned her surroundings with watchful eyes.

Sitting in Ashley's hands, Moley didn't want to betray how well he knew Alexis, but he managed to give her a little wave with his paw, and she closed her eyes in a silent greeting.

The ducklings were still concealed under her. It was amazing to see how she managed to cover all of them with her body. Moley even started to worry (just how did he manage to find new things to worry about?) that she hadn't had any more ducklings since he'd left the day before.

Soon Ashley was called home for lunch and went, returning Moley to the bench with all the toys. Moley felt a little embarrassed that he couldn't tell them much about the ducklings, but soon, to everyone's surprise, they saw Alexis emerging from around the corner.

And behind her...

One, two, three, four...

Moley quickly lost count, but it didn't matter that much. All that mattered was that all the new-born ducklings were hurrying behind their mum, bravely putting one foot in front of the other, trying not to fall behind.

The toys were watching their progress cautiously, knowing that the ducklings were less than a day old! But they followed Alexis in a tight group, sturdily and confidently, little balls of fluff – brown, with darker heads and lighter backs.

Alexis acknowledged the toys with a quick nod and headed straight for the pond.

"She is mad!" exclaimed Owlie. "They are too young to know how to swim!"

Moley saw fear in Rosie's eyes and Rusty started to bark in his small voice.

Alexis, however, did not pay any attention to the commotion on the bench, and went straight into the pond from the shallow bank. The ducklings, without a moment's hesitation, all went after her, one by one.

And they swam!

Oh, how they swam!

They took to water, like...well, like ducks, that's right! Moley had heard the expression "like a duck to water" before, but only now did he understand its full meaning.

The ducklings, less than a day old, were swimming like real experts! He could see that they were enjoying themselves, chasing each other in the silvery sparkly water of the pond, though not yet daring to leave their Mum's side for too long.

From that day onwards Moley's time was filled with all things "ducklings". Watching ducklings, feeding ducklings, playing with ducklings. Yes, he soon became acquainted with them all and played with them often.

The Richards family, from Ashley to Daddy, admired the ducklings very much too. They all (even Mr Richards) talked in high-pitched little voices around the ducklings, as if they themselves were strange oversized birds.

"Just look at them," Mummy would squeak. "So tiny! So cute."

"Happy little fellows," echoed Mr Richards.

Ashley would run to the kitchen to get some food and throw it in the pond for Ludwig and Alexis. First time he did it, he brought some bread with him, but Mummy stopped him: "I'm not sure the ducklings are ready for this type of food", she said and brought a large box of bird seed from the house. They watched with astonishment how Alexis, instead of eating the seeds herself, pushed them gently towards one of her ducklings, as if inviting him to eat.

The ducklings discovered their love for seeds very quickly. Soon, whenever they heard Ashley's voice in the garden, they rushed to him, overtaking their mother and father and surrounded him, waiting for their treat. They got used to Ashley very quickly and not only took food from his hand, but climbed all the way into his lap to get it faster.

Ashley often took Moley with him to feed the ducks.

Moley enjoyed his time with them very much, but he couldn't help but notice that the number of ducklings went down day by day. If at first he couldn't even count them, after a few days he managed to count to ten, then to nine …

Moley couldn't understand what was happening and why the ducks did not show any concern about this. He decided to ask them, but not wishing to upset Alexis with such an indelicate question, Moley waited until one afternoon he spotted Ludwig diving into the pond on his own. Moley called him to the window and asked his question in a hushed voice.

Ludwig's eyes went sad.

"We do not speak of it," was his grave reply.

"What do you mean?" insisted Moley.

"The mystery of the night is a great secret. The night takes its toll."

"Does Alexis know it too?" asked Moley anxiously.

"She is blessed with the happy inability to count," Ludwig replied and went away without a further word.

Despite this last statement, Moley suspected that Alexis knew. He'd noticed her increased anxiety since the ducklings had arrived, and more than once he caught sadness in her eyes when she looked at them.

Moley wasn't the kind of mole to accept such a worrying situation paws down.

"The mystery of the night, honestly!" he muttered under his breath as he rushed back into the house. "I'll show you the mystery! I am not the kind of mole who gives up and doesn't get to the bottom of the secret."

Chapter Fourteen

The Predators

Moley's first instinct would have been, of course, to rush to clever Owlie to discuss the issue. But she still wasn't speaking to him.

And the other toys weren't any help. Rusty and Rosie, the dogs, could only count to four, and that was between them. Rusty knew one and three and Rosie two and four, and together they managed reasonably well, regularly counting each other's paws and the legs of Ashley's bed.

Bronti and Dina couldn't count at all. They insisted that dinosaurs did not count. "Not then, not now," repeated Bronti, very importantly.

Boris could count, albeit only in Russian, and he agreed with Moley that the number of ducklings was decreasing day by day, but he was short of ideas as to why.

Moley felt lost, until next morning he spotted Gordon, the pigeon, picking up bread crumbs left on the lawn after the ducks' breakfast. He noticed with concern that Gordon was limping, his left leg stiff and unbending.

"Good morning, Gordon," shouted Moley from the opened window of Ashley's bedroom. "Are you OK? It looks like you are limping."

Gordon looked up, spread his wings and, with a powerful sound of a sail beating in the wind, flew to the windowsill in one graceful movement.

"Morning, Moley," he said. "Yes. I was attacked last night, but managed to get away."

"Attacked?" Moley was astonished. "Who could attack you in our garden?"

"A weasel," said Gordon.

"A weasel? What's a weasel?"

Moley had never heard such a name and it didn't sound friendly to him.

"A predator," said Gordon.

"What's a predator?"

"There are many of them in the garden at night," Gordon continued. "Some of them might be the distant relatives of Owlie – the owls. But there are others as well. Foxes, rats, weasels... The night is unfriendly and dangerous for all creatures, especially small ones."

Moley, who was quite an anxious creature in any case, was dumbfounded to discover that there was a whole new dangerous thing to worry about, of which he hadn't been aware.

"Could these predators attack the ducklings at night?" he asked Gordon in a trembling voice.

"Most certainly," said Gordon, matter-of-factly.

"Why are you not more anxious about it?" asked Moley.

"I don't worry about things I cannot change," said Gordon. "No point. They are predators, but they also need to eat. Animals are each for themselves, you know. I managed to fight off the weasel, because I am strong and quick. Good for me. But some other night I might be not as lucky. It is a fact of life."

"Well, I am not having this!" exclaimed Moley. "How dare they attack our little, innocent, harmless ducklings! I sat on the nest for weeks, helping them hatch. I did not protect them *before* they were born to abandon them *after* they are born, so that they could become food for some bloodthirsty predators!"

"But what can you do?" asked Gordon.

"I can go and guard them at night."

"But you are small and quite defenceless yourself," said Gordon doubtfully.

"I'll go, nonetheless," replied Moley, determinedly. "I can stay awake the whole night and raise the alarm if someone comes too near."

Moley was very upset that morning and felt completely heart-broken in the afternoon, when he went outside and discovered another

duckling missing. He returned to the house beside himself with worry, threw his high-visibility jacket under the bed and hid himself in a dark corner to think his plan through. The difficulty of being clever is that there is always so much responsibility on your shoulders!

He sighed loudly, and in response heard a little cough followed by Bronti's voice calling from the bed: "Are you alright, Moley?"

"Just fine," replied Moley, shaking his head, wishing to be left alone with his thoughts.

The bed creaked.

"You've not been yourself lately," continued Bronti as he moved to the edge of the bed and looked at Moley from above. "You're not normally the kind of mole to sit on the floor sighing on a fine afternoon like this."

"If you cannot do anything about the ducklings, you'd better try not to think about it at all," suggested Bronti's sister Dina, who had followed her brother and now also peered at Moley from the edge of the bed. They'd both heard Moley's conversation with Gordon that morning and it gave them a sense of unease, of something dangerous creeping into their simple happy lives.

"I can't stop thinking about it," said Moley stubbornly. "And there is no problem in the world that I cannot deal with if I put my mind to it."

With these words he hid his face in his paws, waiting for the night to come, so that he could go and start his guarding duties.

The evening seemed to last forever, but eventually Ashley was tucked in bed, kissed goodnight by his parents, and the lights went off. Moley waited until the whole house went quiet. Then he snuck out of the bedroom, ran downstairs without a sound, and climbed outside through the cat flap.

Chapter Fifteen

The Mystery of the Night

The darkness consumed Moley completely. It was vast, full of new sharp smells, distant bird calls, and other sounds that rang loudly in the stillness of the night. These smells and sounds were unfamiliar to Moley – they sent shivers down his spine. He remained motionless for a while, allowing his eyes to adjust to the darkness, listening and sniffing, getting used to familiar surroundings that seemed so alien to him at this time.

Although after a while Moley could see in the dark perfectly well, he quickly realised that he'd made one crucial mistake – he hadn't told Alexis that he was coming and had no idea where to find her. He could postpone his mission until the next night and return home, but it meant risking the ducklings' lives one more time! Moley decided to press ahead, no matter what. He deduced that Alexis most likely would be sleeping by the pond, and therefore he needed to go to the front of the house and to go around the pond in the hope of finding her.

He set off. But even though he tiptoed around the house, and negotiated the lawns and flowerbeds as carefully as he could, he managed to catch a bunch of his fur on a blackberry thorn and got soaked up to his waist in a puddle. Shaking the water off himself, he noticed another thing – in his hurry to get out he'd forgotten to put on his high-visibility jacket! All in all, the whole expedition had not started well, but Moley wasn't the kind of mole who turned back.

After much rambling in the tall grass by the pond, he spotted Alexis on the far side, sleeping with her head buried in the feathers on her back. The ducklings were nowhere to be seen, until Moley realised that all eight of them (and they were much bigger now than when they were first born), were hiding underneath her body. Moley was always amazed by Alexis' ability to hide all her babies this way. Ludwig didn't seem to be around.

'And he calls himself a father!' thought Moley in a judgemental voice.

Silently, Moley moved towards Alexis. He didn't want to wake up the ducklings and made every effort not to create any noise. For this very reason he decided not to speak, and, once he was near enough, stretched his paw and patted Alexis gently on her side.

He wasn't ready for what had happened next!

Alexis jumped, flapped her wings and, with one swift movement of her head, caught Moley and threw him into the pond.

Moley flew high and far, and landed in the middle of the pond, almost silently, for he was soft and very light. He was so taken aback by what had happened, that he didn't even have time to feel scared.

At first he floated on the surface of the dark pond, and quite liked the sensation. Paws stretched out like a star, he thought proudly how he'd managed to do both flying and swimming in one night, not noticing that his fur was gradually getting soggier and heavier, pulling him down into the dark, still waters of the pond.

When he noticed, he panicked.

"Help..." squeaked Moley, softly at first, then louder the second time.

"HELP!"

His whole body was under the surface now. He kept his nose above water (just!) but didn't dare to open his mouth again. Fear gripped his mind and all he could do was to push his nose up, all his senses dulled.

He didn't hear the loud call of a wood pigeon in the tree above, followed by the heavy splash of a duck landing on the water. He didn't see a strong yellow beak reaching down for him. He didn't feel himself being pulled out of the water and delivered to the safety of the grassy bank. He only came to several minutes later, lying on his back – two beaks pressing on his chest in turns.

He coughed a little and sat up.

He saw Ludwig and Alexis right in front of him, Alexis looking embarrassed, Ludwig – very cross.

"You see, woman? You almost killed Moley, our saviour!" said Ludwig, angrily.

"I am so sorry!" Alexis said through tears. "I am used to protecting my children at night. I didn't have time to check out who our attacker was and I wouldn't recognise you at night, not without your high-visibility jacket anyway!"

The little ducklings were all here too. They pecked at Moley's feet with their tiny beaks and it was, actually, quite ticklish. Moley shivered and giggled. Then giggled some more. And not long after, they were all laughing out loud together with a sense of massive relief.

That night Moley slept with the ducks, warmed by the eight fluffy bodies of his duckling-friends, and the soft feathers of their Mother-Duck. Ludwig stood nearby, keeping watch.

Chapter Sixteen

The Great Storm

When the morning came, Moley woke up and discovered that his body was still too heavy with water for him to move. It didn't worry him much, for he didn't need to be anywhere in particular that day. In fact, he felt slightly relieved that he didn't have to spend any time in Ashley's bedroom with Owlie still not talking to him, and the other toys too scared to upset her. He felt a little guilty for not wanting to go back and tried to justify it to himself: 'They won't even notice I am not there. Nobody likes me there anymore...' It was quite unfair, but at that moment Moley believed it to be true and looked forward to spending the whole day by the pond.

It was a nice day. The sun was shining, the pond glittered like a mirror, the air was full of birds' chatter. All troubles of the previous night forgotten, Moley sat on the grass, watching the ducklings chasing each other around the pond. The little fellows were still so light that they managed to run on top of the shiny surface, pushing the water beneath them with their webbed feet.

Alexis too watched from nearby, never taking her eyes off them. After a while she called them all to the bank and they settled next to Moley, drying their little wings and cleaning their fluffy feathers in the sunshine. It was a good time to talk to Alexis about the dangers of the night. To Moley's utter astonishment, the Mother-Duck actually couldn't count her ducklings, just as Ludwig had said, and never referred to any individual duckling by name. They were all just "ducklings" to her and she only perceived them as a group. Neither Ludwig nor Alexis wanted to talk about the night predators, as if daylight made all the dangers disappear.

Feeling too tired to insist, Moley decided that he would be coming out every night to keep watch over them, wearing his high-visibility jacket. He was sure that his bright yellow jacket with its glow-in-the-dark stripes on the back would be sufficient to scare any predators away. Having reached this conclusion, he lay close to Alexis' warm side and fell asleep on the sunny bank, feeling quite contented.

He was awakened by a terrible sound of howling wind. The sky had turned dark, tightly packed with low-hanging clouds, the young trees around the pond bent low to the ground, and although it was not raining yet, it was clear that rain wasn't very far away.

"Moley, we need to hide in a more sheltered place," shouted Alexis over the growling of the wind. "The ducklings are too light. They might be swept away."

"Go," shouted Moley back to her. "Go and leave me, I'll be alright."

"I'll come back for you!" cried Ludwig.

Protecting the ducklings with their bodies, Alexis and Ludwig herded them slowly towards a gunnera plant at the far end of the pond. This plant had leaves so big that they could hide Ashley, never mind the family of ducks. The leaves reached the ground in a wide circle and the whole plant looked like a giant green dome, creating a perfect shelter.

As the ducks disappeared under the enormous gunnera leaves, the low clouds in the sky could not hold back the rain anymore – they gave way and the rain came down in sheets. Moley's furry body, that had just started to dry, was soaked through again in moments and became even heavier than before. He could hardly move.

Moley knew that staying on the muddy, slippery bank in the middle of the storm all by himself was a bad idea, and tried to move towards the house. Resisting wind and rain with all his might, he crawled towards the back of the house, pressed hard to the ground with the weight of water in his fur. He hadn't made much progress, when a strong beak lifted him off the ground – Ludwig had returned for him, just as he'd promised. By now Moley was so heavy with water that Ludwig couldn't fly with the weight, which was just as well, because the wind was getting stronger by the minute. No bird was airborne in this weather, they all hid in cracks and niches wherever they could find them.

Ludwig walked, moving each foot with tremendous effort, dragging Moley with him. His progress towards the house was very slow, but it was still much faster than Moley could have crawled himself. They could see the back door in the distance when the sky split open and a bolt of blinding light erupted over their heads. The light was quickly followed by the most deafening sound, as if a whole load of boulders had rolled over them.

For a moment Ludwig stopped dead and dropped Moley from his grasp, but as soon as the thunder was over, he picked his friend up again and continued towards the back door with renewed vigour. He wanted to deliver Moley to safety as soon as he could and return to his family.

Their journey seemed to take forever, but eventually they reached the back door. The wind here, behind the house, had subsided, and the porch over the door protected them from the rain, if only a little. Moley tried to lift his body up to the cat flap, but he was too heavy for that. It was frustrating. He was so close to home, but yet another hurdle kept him away from it.

"You must go, Ludwig," said Moley. "I'll hide between the flower pots here and wait until morning. Mrs Richards is bound to come out of the back door. She'll pick me up."

"Are you sure?" asked Ludwig, but Moley could tell that he was happy with the plan.

"I am absolutely, unequivocally sure," he replied, hoping that a big word would impress Ludwig and make him agree to go. It worked.

"Stay safe," said Ludwig with a nod and turned his feet back towards the pond.

Moley found a relatively dry corner between the flowerpots and squeezed himself tightly into the narrow gap, so that the wind could not reach him easily. He was extremely grateful to Ludwig and ashamed of himself for having judged him so harshly before. Ludwig was a good father and a good friend, after all. He was there for his family and for him, Moley, when he was most needed. Moley had learnt another lesson: not to be too hasty with his judgements! How many more lessons would he have to learn to become as good a friend to those around him as he wanted to be?

He was sitting there in the darkness, listening to the howling wind, and the roof tiles rattling above his head, mulling over these thoughts, losing track of time. The lightning lit up the garden with its unnaturally white light from time to time, making every single blade of grass clearly visible. The lightning always came unexpectedly, but the thunder followed closely and Moley soon created a game for himself, counting the seconds between the two, and trying to predict what it would be the next time. All in all, he was bearing his solitude quite reasonably. Until...

Until in a brief moment of the next flash of lightning, he saw something that made his insides freeze with fear. A tiny ball of feathers and fluff was being carried by the wind away from the pond, in the direction of the house where Moley sat motionless. A duckling!

The duckling rolled past Moley and came to a stop a few steps away, under a wooden bench.

What was Moley to do?!

In his mind there were no doubts. He needed to save the little one.

Without a moment's hesitation, Moley pushed himself out from his hiding place and started crawling in the direction of the bench, reasonably fast at first, desperate in his attempt to save the little fellow, but more and more slowly with every next push, his body soaking up water from the ground, making him heavier and heavier.

Moley was just a couple of steps from the bench when he felt his strength leaving him completely, and a realisation dawned on him that he might not be able to move any further...

It was a terrible feeling – to be so close, to be able to make out the duckling's shape in the darkness under the bench but not be able to help.

Tears of desperation and frustration filled Moley's eyes, when suddenly he felt a light touch on his shoulder and the end of a rope being pushed into his paws.

To his astonishment Moley saw Rusty and Rosie, holding tight to each other, a piece of rope in Rusty's mouth.

"The duckling," said Moley feebly, "he's under the bench."

Without a word Rusty went to the bench with the end of the rope, while Rosie stayed with Moley and secured the middle of the rope around his chest.

In a few moments Moley heard Rusty's bark: "Pull!"

"Pull!" shouted Rosie in the direction of the back door and, turning his head with an effort, Moley saw Bronti and Dina halfway to the back door, holding the rope with a look of determination on their little faces.

"Pull!" Their voices repeated the command.

"Raz, dva, tri," Moley heard Boris's call. And a strong tug got the whole chain of animals moving.

With every pull the rope was moving, bringing them all closer to safety.

First Bronti and Dina disappeared through the cat flap, then it was Moley and Rosie's turn, and finally came Rusty, holding onto the rope with his teeth, the little duckling in his paws.

Moley looked around the kitchen – and saw Boris, his arms outstretched, a big smile on his face, and behind him – Owlie! Moley's

112

eyes met hers, and for the first time in weeks she didn't turn away, looking directly back at him. Moley's small eyes blinked very fast, fighting back unexpected tears, and hope rose in his sodden chest. Did this mean Owlie had finally forgiven him? Were they going to be friends again?

Chapter Seventeen

After the Storm

Boris covered them all with a big fluffy towel he'd pulled off the radiator. It was Ashley's pool towel, he always left it to dry in the kitchen after his swimming lessons. Owlie sat next to the towel, cradling the little duckling in her wings.

"Quack you," said the duckling to her.

"Thank him," hooted Owlie and pointed at Moley's pink nose sticking out from the folds of a towel.

"I think, Moley," whispered Boris, "we've found the duckling that should be named after you."

A sense of safety and security enveloped Moley, and he collapsed into his friends' warm embrace, finally succumbing to fatigue after his colossal ordeal.

All through the night the storm raged on outside, but Moley and his friends slept soundly, wrapped up in their towel, the duckling cuddled up under Owlie's wing, and only Boris stayed awake, keeping watch until the storm was over and everything was quiet again.

With the first ray of sunshine he woke everyone and for a while they sat in the warm kitchen, talking in hushed voices.

Moley told them about his adventures of the night before last, then they all turned to the duckling: "How did you get lost?"

"I runs away," said duckling, guiltily. "I sits with others and then – BOOM, BOOM! I scare, I wants my Dad, quack, quack, he – big and strong. I runs."

They couldn't get much more out of him, but the picture was clear enough. Scared by the thunder he'd lost his head, and ran away in panic to find his Dad. The wind had picked up his light little body and blew it all the way to the house where, thankfully, Moley and the others had spotted him.

"But what I don't understand," said Moley, turning to other toys, "is how *did* you spot him – in the middle of the night, at the height of the storm? How *did* you know that your help was needed?"

"It was Owlie," said Rusty. "She'd kept an eye on you all this time."

Owlie lowered her head: "I did, I admit."

"Ever since you'd discovered that ducklings were disappearing at night, I knew you wouldn't rest until you found a way to save them. You are not the kind of mole to give up easily. I watched you secretly, in case you needed my help. The day before your night expedition you were particularly agitated. I noticed that you'd thrown your high-visibility jacket under the bed, and sat the whole afternoon in the corner. I knew you were brewing up a plan. My only regret is that I didn't stop you when you sneaked out that night. I was still upset with you and was determined not to talk to you, but now I know how selfish I was. I could have stopped you, I could have given you some advice, I could have told you to pick up your jacket. But... I was too proud. And my pride nearly cost you your life. I am sorry."

Moley knew that it must not have been easy for Owlie to apologise to him, especially in such an open way, in front of all the toys, in front of the little duckling too. He could recognise graciousness when he saw it. Owlie was, indeed, a very noble bird!

"Owlie, I need to apologise too!" he exclaimed. "I know I hurt your feelings that day by the nest. I am truly, truly sorry."

"I know you are!" said Owlie, passionately. "You've said it so many times! But my pride was the thing that prevented me from forgiving you! The fault is mine and mine alone."

"Here now, Owlie!" protested Moley. "I was proud too. I thought I would be able to tackle the dangers of the night all by myself! I was too big-headed!"

"But I was too stubborn..."

"Ahem," Boris interrupted their heated discussion. "Can we agree that you BOTH acted like big-headed fools and move on with the story?"

Owlie choked on her next word. Moley was just about to laugh, but caught himself in time and looked at Owlie quizzically. She understood his unspoken question and laughed aloud herself. It was the first time the toys had seen her laughing. It was quite a spectacle – she puffed up like a big ball, her eyes became narrow like slits, and she beat her sides with her wings, hooting: "Ooph, ooph, ooph".

"Arr-ha-ha!" laughed Boris.

"Woof-foof-foof," laughed the dogs.

"Heeee-heee-hee," joined in the dinosaurs.

"Eeeeh-he-he." Moley rolled on his back, overcome.

And even the little duckling, though not having understood anything from the conversation, joined the fun happily: "Quack, yak, yak!"

When they had laughed their fill, Owlie told the rest of her story. How, knowing that Moley had gone to look for Alexis, she'd sat on the windowsill in front of the drawn curtain, and scanned the grounds with her large and used-to-darkness eyes. How she spotted Moley eventually and saw him approaching Alexis. How to her horror she saw Alexis throwing Moley into the pond and then settle herself back to sleep, not knowing what she'd done.

"You were lucky, Moley, that Gordon, ever since his incident with the weasel, had decided to spend his nights on the trellis right under Ashley's window. I tapped on the window with all my might and managed to wake him up."

To Gordon's credit, he'd understood at once what Owlie was trying to tell him. Without wasting any time, he took off and woke up Ludwig, who slept just a little distance from Alexis and the ducklings. Ludwig dived into the pond and saved Moley just in time.

Moley was astonished.

"Owlie, you saved my life! You saved my life even though you were cross with me, even though your feelings were so hurt!"

"My feelings…" said Owlie. "You see, my feelings were no longer hurt at all by that stage. My feelings were quite the opposite to what they were before. I was fed up with this confrontation, but didn't know how to end it without losing face. I wanted to be friends with you again. I just didn't have the faintest idea how to go about it without admitting that I was wrong not to forgive you for so long. And I never like to admit that I am wrong, you know..."

"I know," replied Moley and worried that he'd said the wrong thing again. "I mean, I know, because I am the same –"

"My friends, you've made mistakes. It happens," Boris interrupted again. "Let's forget about the past. Tell us what happened next, Owlie."

"There's not that much to tell," said Owlie. "When Moley hadn't returned the next day, I didn't worry, because Gordon kept me updated on the situation every other hour. I knew that Ashley was worried, but he wasn't too upset, for he believed he'd just left Moley somewhere in the house and was going to have a good search for him at the weekend. I was sure that Moley would return home by then."

"But when the storm started, I knew it meant trouble," she continued. "I kept watching through the window that was covered with streaks of water by then, and even my sharp eyes were often mistaken in trying to judge the situation outside. Gordon couldn't help, he was hiding in a large hole inside the oak tree with some other birds."

"Eventually I saw Ludwig carrying Moley towards the house. I knew that Moley would not be able to climb through the cat flap by himself with all that water inside his fur, so I decided to organise a little rescue expedition. I knew there was a long rope under Ashley's bed, it had been left there since the time when Ashley used it to swing on the tree. I got Boris to find it and carry it down. We all followed."

"It took us a while to organise ourselves and get downstairs," said Boris, taking over from Owlie, "but in the end we did it. I was holding one end of the rope, Rusty and Rosie, another. Owlie was our commander." He pronounced it KOMANDIRRRR, with a long RRRR at the end, which sounded very impressive.

"I felt that we needed Bronti and Dina to hold the rope in the middle, to give the whole chain more weight, to fight the wind," explained Owlie.

"And we started climbing out!" exclaimed Rusty, who was very excited and wanted to say his bit. "We thought you would be right by the door, but you were not there! Good job I could pick up your scent, even in all that rain – it was very faint, but it was there..."

"We followed the scent," said Rosie, not wanting to be left out either, "and felt very scared."

"But we were so glad that we had the rope," barked Rusty.

"When we found you, we thought that was it, but then you told us about the duckling..." said Rosie.

"Yes, we didn't know about the duckling!" agreed Rusty.

From that point Moley knew the story himself. But he felt bad that Bronti and Dina hadn't been given a chance to tell their bit. He turned towards them, but they just smiled at him happily, their large eyes full of pride. They didn't talk much, these dinosaurs, but they were always there for you if you needed them.

The story was over and the whole nightmare behind them. All that was left to do was to return the duckling to his parents and go back to Ashley's bedroom before he awoke.

The small toys and the duckling went outside again through the cat flap, Boris and Owlie watching from inside.

The morning was bright and fresh. The garden, thoroughly washed by the night's rain, sparkled like a room after a spring clean: the stone paths shining like silver, every leaf on the trees gleaming with the brightest green, the flowers filling the air with delightful smells. The birds had just started their cheerful song, celebrating safe delivery from the thunderstorm.

It was all so beautiful that Moley and his friends stopped still for a moment, taking in the loveliness of the day. But they didn't have much time. They needed to hurry.

They walked with the little duckling around the house to the French window, where his family usually enjoyed their breakfast in the morning. And, to everyone's surprise and delight, there they all were – Alexis and Ludwig and their children. They'd survived the storm and were over the moon with joy to see Moley and the runaway duckling, both safe and sound.

There was no time for sharing their stories, so after a few exclamations of gratitude they parted: the ducks heading towards the pond, and the toys – back to the house.

"Take care of yourself, Moley-two," shouted Rosie to the duckling, as she turned the corner of the house. That was how the duckling got his name.

Moley and his friends made their way upstairs (Moley had to be helped by Boris, because he was still too heavy to lift himself up from step to step), quietly entered Ashley's bedroom, and one-by-one found their favourite spot on his bed. Moley, who was too wet and too heavy to climb on the bed, had settled himself in the corner. So, when the family woke up, there was no hint of the night's adventures, except for the dirty towel on the kitchen floor. But who pays attention to such an unimportant thing?

Epilogue

From that day forward, the toys went to look after the ducklings every night. They agreed to go in pairs, so that one could always help the other, should something unexpected happen. Bronti went with Dina, Rusty with Rosie, and Moley – to his utter delight – with Owlie! Even if it was very difficult for her to push her large body through the cat flap and back, she practised and practised and eventually learnt to do it with a certain degree of grace and some pushing power from Boris.

Their night vigils paid off. No more ducklings disappeared in the night, and the predators quickly learnt that this family of ducks was protected and they stopped coming into the Richards's garden.

For the first time in his life Moley realised that a responsibility shared is a responsibility halved. No, not halved! It was actually smashed into many pieces, as many pieces as friends involved in performing the task! And each piece became smaller and much more manageable than the one, huge, undivided responsibility. Moley felt as if the heavy load was not quite lifted off his shoulders, but shared among many-many shoulders, so that carrying it wasn't such a burden anymore.

But a few days later, his newly found peace of mind was presented with another challenge.

One day Ashley came home early, swiftly ran upstairs, threw his school bag into the corner and jumped on his bed – arms stretched, smiling from ear to ear.

"Holidays!" he shouted at the top of his voice.

From Ashley's behaviour Moley could see that it was happy news, and his fellow toys looked delighted as well.

"Ashley will stay home with us every day now," whispered Rosie into Moley's ear.

That was brilliant news! Moley swelled with happiness and anticipation of the many wonderful adventures in the garden they would have with Ashley. And his expectations came true, until... a few days later a suitcase appeared on the floor of Ashley's bedroom, and he started quickly packing all sort of things into it. Socks, pants, T-shirts, shorts, a toothbrush and toothpaste, binoculars, pens and pencils.

"Travelling! We are going to go travelling!" he explained to his toys, excitedly.

Travelling?

That was Moley's greatest dream. But he wasn't sure that Ashley would take any of his toys with him, let alone him, Moley, in particular. The suitcase wasn't that big. Plus, Moley wasn't sure that leaving the ducks at this particular moment would be such a good idea. They were still vulnerable and needed guarding at night. And yet he wanted to travel. Really, REALLY wanted to travel!

Going to and fro in his thinking while Ashley was packing his suitcase, Moley could not make a decision. But when Ashley looked away, Moley pulled on his high-visibility jacket, just in case.

However, soon Ashley closed the lid and turned the dials of the automatic lock on his case, not packing any toys into it, and Moley decided to accept this as a sign. 'I am not going anywhere and it is fine. I am needed here. This is my place.'

He turned his head to the wall, with a mixture of disappointment and resignation in his chest. He didn't want the other toys to see that he was upset.

Ashley was about to leave the room, his suitcase in one hand, his small rucksack in the other.

"You – be good, all of you," he said, turning to his toys. "I'll be back in no time, and maybe even with a new friend for you!"

And then, matter-of-factly: "Are you ready to go, Moley? Let's go!"

With these words he picked up Moley, and settled him into the front pocket of his rucksack in such a way that Moley's head and front paws were free and he could see everything.

Moley's breath stuck in his throat with surprise!

He just managed to wave to his friends –

And they were out of the room!

Now his destiny was decided in favour of travelling, Moley started panicking.

'I haven't left any instructions for anybody. I haven't had another conversation with Alexis about safety, I haven't planned a proper guarding schedule...' His thoughts ran in circles in his head, chasing each other.

Sitting in the rucksack on the back seat of the car while Ashley helped his parents to pack the boot, Moley looked out of the rolled-down window with a heavy heart. When he saw Gordon the Pigeon, landing on the porch roof, Moley called out to him.

"Gordon, thank goodness! I am going away, but I haven't arranged anything to make sure everyone is safe in my absence. Can you please tell Alexis–"

"Moley!" Gordon interrupted him, firmly. "Stop! Look around, think back. You've done everything you could to ensure everyone's safety. The toys and animals are all working together and helping each other. Because of you. Now it is time for you to trust your friends. To trust their judgement and their ability to work together. And there is no reason to doubt their ability. You've done well, Moley. You can go with Ashley and enjoy your trip. You deserve it. All will be well."

And Moley realised that Gordon was right. This home was in good hands – his friends would look after it and each other. If he could trust them with his life, he could trust them with anything.

The Richardses were in the car. The engine started. Ashley took Moley out of the rucksack and brought him to the window, so he could see better. The porch, and Gordon on top of it, were slowly moving away.

Moley waved.

He knew – all would be well.

Acknowledgements:

So many people helped me and encouraged me throughout the creation of this story, and, I would like to offer my heartfelt thanks to:

Susannah Waters and all members of **The Fraudian Society** for being my first readers, editors and critics

Alison Larkin for her amazing *Just Do It* inspirational speech over some delicious Thai curry

Leo and Victoria – my first children readers and reviewers and their Mum, **Anna**

Linda and Ester Silver for selling to us Moley and Dina at a school fair, and for being lovely people, not at all like Lorna and her Mum

Cassandra Grafton, for helping, reading, listening, encouraging and supporting me all the way

Margaret Bremner for her absolutely superb and thorough proofreading and counting ducklings from page to page with outstanding accuracy

My parents, **Boris and Valentina**, for supporting me in this journey and lending our bear his wonderful Russian name, Boris, that is completely unrelated to the current British Prime Minister

Elena Tarnovskaya for helping me with the cover in the most reassuring and confidence–inducing manner

Carol Wellart for not just being an amazing artist, but for listening and making sure that every single illustration is just right, it's been an absolute pleasure and delight working with you

And last, but never least, **Paul and Sasha**, for pestering and nagging me to continue with this book, checking it again and again, reading and re-reading, putting up with my worries and insecurities, and being there for me ALWAYS.

THANK YOU!

Readers' Reviews

I loved reading about Moley and his adventures! I'm so glad he was taken out of his box and to a new family. I hope to have my own Moley one day, so we can go on adventures too.

Gabrielle aged 5 years and 7 months

A mole like no other

This book is about a toy mole who found a new family.

I really like this book because its a really good story to listen to before bed time. The only thing was that mum had to stop reading somewhere in the middle of the chapter because my five year old sister would fall asleep so I would have to wait next evening.

I liked all the characters but my favourite one is Moley. Moley is cute, brave, friendly and always wants to help. I would like to have a friend like Moley!

Leon M

8 years old
13/12/20

Wonderful, sensitive and charming. And – very funny! I found myself reading it aloud.

Geoffrey Hall, Actor

My favourite character was Moley because he was funny and helped people when he could. The best part of the book was when Moley and Owlie were arguing about whose fault it was, each blaming themselves, and they were told to stop - which was hilarious. If you make another book, I would like to see what happened on the holiday. **Rhys, 10 years old**

I loved it!
I liked to look at the pictures while my mummy read the story. I loved all the characters but my favourite was Alexis because she is a good mummy. It was funny when Moley saw his own reflection and got angry at himself. I liked the bit where Moley was chosen to go on holiday. I would like to join Moley on another adventure. Skye, 5 years old

> I loved the story of moley and his friends. He is such a helpful and friendly mole. We are so glad he found a new home and made lots of friends! It was fun to read this story with my mam and sister.
>
> Keira, aged 7

A funny and engaging stuffed mole enriches the lives of everyone around him, whilst always on the lookout for new friends and experiences! We loved how Moley could be quite serious and earnest, but find fun and enjoyment in every situation. All the characters are delightful, adding colour and excitement to the tale.

Children's logic and understanding of the world perfectly expressed by childlike toys and their animal friends. The story worked for both our kids. The story was exciting and charming for younger children, while the older ones can gain more from the language and characters. The language is reminiscent of the stories we read as children but with a modern twist. It has created a safe space for our children at a time when it is needed the most.

Lyndsay (aged 37 ☺) & Si (aged 38 ☺), parents

I am convinced it will become a children's classic.

Cass Grafton, Author

Write Your Own Review Here:

···
···
···
···
···
···
···
···
···
···

Thank you and well done!

About the Author:

Julia B. Grantham lives in the South of England with her husband, son, two cats, Moley, Owlie and all the other toys that make their appearance in this book; with ducks and pigeons in the garden, chickens across the road, as well as rabbits, squirrels, pheasants and deer, who visit often and hope also to make it into a book one day soon. Julia is a medical doctor and a training consultant, but books are her passion. She is a Harry Potter fanatic, an Ambassador for the *Jane Austen Literacy Foundation*, a writer and illustrator of Jane Austen-inspired travel fiction, and now – an author of her first book for children.

Julia's Facebook profile:

Search for **J.B. Grantham**

Direct Link: https://www.facebook.com/J.B.Grantham.Author/

You can become friends with Moley and get to know him in his day-to-day life on his Facebook Page:

https://www.facebook.com/AMoleLikeNoOther

About the Illustrator:

Carol Wellart is an award-winning artist and a book illustrator from Czechia. She's a co-author of the first illustrated wolf chronicle *'Wolves are coming'* and her work was published in American magazines such as the *Spirituality & Health Magazine, International Wolf,* and *The Orion.*

Carol prefers creating images with the themes of wildlife, nature, and literary characters, so when Julia and Carol joined forces to create the visuals for this book it was a union of kindred spirits!

Carol's Website:

https://carolwellart.com/artist

Find Moley on Facebook and become his friend!

Moley and Friends

@AMoleLikeNoOther · Book series

www.facebook.com/AMoleLikeNoOther/

Made in the USA
Monee, IL
27 June 2021

72393229R00074